THE
ZERO KNOT

K. Z. SNOW

Dreamspinner Press

Published by
Dreamspinner Press
382 NE 191st Street #88329
Miami, FL 33179-3899, USA
http://www.dreamspinnerpress.com/

The Zero Knot

Cover Art by Anne Cain   annecain.art@gmail.com
Cover Design by Mara McKennen

ISBN: 978-1-61372-204-6

Printed in the United States of America
First Edition
October 2011

eBook edition available
eBook ISBN: 978-1-61372-205-3

PROLOGUE

THEIR voices, audible through the cracked-open bedroom door, came from the living room.

"What the *hell* has your kid done to my son?"

"If you're referring to Jesse, it appears all he's done is fall in love."

"What are you talking about? Do you realize how insane that sounds? They're *boys*, Jim. They're two teenaged *boys*."

"Have you looked at them lately? Listened to them? They're not boys. They're very capable young men."

Not silence. Not quite. Tom's breathing punched ragged holes in the stillness. "All right. Two young men. *Males*. And from what I've *heard*, they sure as hell aren't friends anymore."

"Of course they are. They're the best of friends."

A mumbled "Oh my God," incredulous. "I hope and pray they haven't taken this too far. How can you be so casual about it? Are you like that too?"

"Like what?" A flat question, no inflection. "In love? I wish."

More silence, followed by, "My boy just got out of jail. Some depraved liar he used to trust put him there. That experience made him vulnerable. Now someone else he trusts—someone he sees as, I don't know, some kind of savior—has taken advantage of his weakness and convinced him to lie to himself. To *live* a lie." Tom's voice rose, buoyed by a furious indignation. "But that's one profane savior who manages to convince a perfectly normal boy that he's—"

"I think you need to stop now."

"Are you threatening me?"

"No. If anything, I'm admitting I *can't* threaten you. I'm too old to throw you out of my house. So I'm suggesting you just go home, cool down, and think. At some time in the future, talk to your son. More important, listen to him. He can teach you all about lies, and the consequences of lies. And if you don't listen, Tom, that door he's walking through right now, the one that leads to adulthood and his own life, will be closed to you forever."

"Go get him." A surly demand, growled as much as spoken. "I know he's here."

"No, I won't do that. You're not ready yet. Besides, he's his own man now. Neither one of us can make him do anything."

"I don't know what's gotten into you, Jim."

"I'll tell you what. The realization that both our sons have learned a damn sight more this past summer than *we* have in years."

CHAPTER 1

THE waxy stink from a half-dozen cheap, sputtering candles vied with the odor of weed already skunking the air in Brandon Nygaard's basement. Jess Bonner tried to wave the tendrils of smoke away from his face. He was sitting on the floor, at the opposite side of the coffee table from the couch, so he was really getting doused. Silently, and for the millionth time, he cursed the dogshit quality of Chinese imports.

The Nygaards could easily afford stuff that didn't come from China's largest colony, Walmart, but they kept that stuff upstairs and held it in reserve for "real" company. Yankee and Candleworks candles would never shed their heavenly scents over the teenagers who assembled in the basement, out of parental sight... and mind.

Well, Jess supposed, that was one of the prices of privacy. The four members of the Domino Club could party however they chose in their subterranean hideaway. Bran's parents didn't much give a crap what went on, as long as they weren't held liable.

Tonight the partying didn't amount to much, even though Bran's parents and younger sister were visiting relatives in Allouez. Everybody being stoned combined with being wrung out at the end of the workweek didn't make for a high-velocity get-together.

Jess again flapped a hand as he grimaced in disgust. Smoke from the charred wicks kept slithering up his nostrils.

"Someone fart?" Bran asked, glancing up from the joint he

3

was rolling. His desultory smirk complemented his low-hung eyelids.

Tomby, the only girl in the group, was quick to protest her innocence. She sat beside Bran on the couch, one hand resting possessively on his hunched back.

"It's the candles," Jess said.

"They don't burn very clean, do they?" Mig, who sat cross-legged next to Jess, reached for the worst offender and neatly snuffed it with a pinch. "Is that better?" The hint of a smile played over his lips, but he didn't let the hint become a statement. He rarely gave in to a smile.

Jess did, often and easily. "That should help. Thanks."

Mig—real name Dylan Finch—had a mild voice that matched his mild manner, and large, soft brown eyes that matched both. He seemed more like some sword-and-sorcery gaming dweeb than the ace welder and Vietnam War history buff that he was. In fact, everything about him breathed contradiction.

Mig had been a shy kid when he, Jess, Bran, and Tomby were growing up together on Sunrise Street in Cold Harbor. Now, fresh out of high school and a week away from his eighteenth birthday, Mig was shy still. That he'd even become part of the Domino Club had been something of a shock to Jess, and probably to Bran and Tomby too. The club, as absurd as it was, hadn't been designed to accommodate wallflowers.

"Music?" Tomby said, looking across the coffee table at Mig and Jess. She obviously didn't want to break the circuit she was trying to establish with Bran.

"I'll get it," Jess said, touching Mig's leg. "I owe you." He got up and ambled toward the entertainment center.

Tomby was a real piece of work. At sixteen, she was the youngest in the group, but that didn't stop her from being imperious and pushy and something of a mathematics wunderkind. Although she'd developed an awe-inspiring rack by the time she was thirteen, her family had always called her a tomboy—hence, the nickname. She'd happily embraced it and thrown off Dominga.

Tomby was the one who'd come up with the whole secret-society notion as well as the Domino Club's name. She'd done so when the four neighborhood friends had begun to feel—and, in tentative steps, talk about—their burgeoning sexuality. One self-conscious confession had followed another.

None of the friends, it turned out, was exclusively attracted to the opposite gender.

Following Tomby's lead, they declared themselves bisexual.

But none of them, it turned out, was being completely honest.

Given his train of thought, Jess decided to put on an Elton John CD, part of the older parental collection. The newer parental collection was, like the quality candles, kept upstairs. Bran the hipster kept his music segregated, as if he didn't want the mold from those oldies tainting his discs.

After Jess tucked Elton into the player, he flipped indifferently through both sets of offerings. He came across an Adam Lambert disc, thought again how he'd like to do or be done by the guy, and went on.

More pot smoke, thick and pungent, drifted sluggishly around his head. Tomby's voice cut through the music as she talked about bringing one of her female friends into the group.

"I'd have to check her out," Bran said. "A three- or foursome might be a nice change of pace once in a while."

Suddenly and irrevocably, Jess knew he wanted to distance himself from this silliness. The Domino Club hadn't expanded his sexual horizons much, if at all, and he was sick of the posturing. Besides, bringing more girls into the group wasn't a prospect he welcomed with enthusiasm. He didn't want to piss away his last months before college pretending to be something he wasn't.

5

Jess had known all along he was a thoroughbred queer—strictly gay, nothing fuzzy, flexible, or fluid about it. Even Tomby's magnificent breasts were little more than a curiosity to him, like those silicone-filled boob vests the queens on *RuPaul's Drag Race* sometimes wore. The idea of touching Tomby's "girls"—something Jess couldn't bring himself to do, primarily because she was a minor but also because, well, he had no desire to—made him think of biology class, of poking at a fish's air bladder or the eyeball of a cow. Real passion, he suspected, didn't have that glaze of clinical detachment.

His reaction to naked guys in magazines and porn flicks had clued him in about that. The little bit of fooling around he'd done with Bran and other guys had clued him in more forcefully. But the strongest clue of all came through certain looks he exchanged with Mig. Something inside Jess crackled and melted, drizzling from his chest to his groin, when Mig's black-lashed eyes met his. And it got worse as they got older, as maturity lent depth to Mig's gaze, resonance to his voice, and luscious definition to his long, lean muscles.

Mig was a thoroughbred too. Jess was sure of it. Why *they* hadn't fooled around together was part of the mystery that was Mig and a source of boundless frustration to Jess. He hadn't made any advances simply because Mig hadn't encouraged any, and Jess didn't want to alienate a childhood friend.

Oh well. Chemistry wasn't always mutual.

He resumed his seat on the floor and took the rapidly dwindling joint from Bran's fingers. As Elton wailed in the background about someone saving his life, Mig rose and headed for the bathroom. Tomby kept up her not-so-subtle seduction of Bran, but he seemed oblivious.

Bran... now *he* was harder to peg. Although he talked about the girls he banged and had plenty of feel-up sessions with Tomby, he was strangely lackadaisical about his hetero hookups. Jess figured Bran might be the only one of them who actually *was*

6

bisexual but likely had a preference for guys.

And Tomby? Hell, she was probably just a precocious middle child trying to set herself apart from her four sisters. Throughout high school, Jess couldn't help noticing how many girls feigned lesbianism or bisexuality to get attention. In Tomby's case, it was Bran's attention she coveted most.

So the Domino Club was built on a foundation of bullshit, basically, and there was nothing unique or meaningful about it. Plenty of other kids pretended to be ambisexual or omnisexual or whatever the hell kind of I'll-try-anything sexual. They figured it projected the image of some super-cool Freebird who'd fly anywhere, try anything. It was a trendy game, not a lifestyle, and the players were in subconscious agreement about its outcome: sometime in the near future, they'd all be married with children, and they'd look back with varying degrees of shame or bemusement on their same-sex experimentation.

Mig returned from the bathroom and once again sank to his spot on the floor, his knee brushing Jess's leg as he got situated. Even minor contact was making Jess squirmy tonight. He didn't have too many opportunities for hookups, so temptation was a more or less constant, annoying companion.

He still hadn't fully come out to anybody. Being openly gay in small-town America didn't carry the same cachet as being bi. It was riskier too. Declaring your homosexuality could put a target on your back. You weren't a Freebird who'd soon be earthbound. You were an alien, and you'd never be anything else.

"Excited about your birthday party?" Jess asked Mig.

"Which one?"

"How many are you *having*?" Tomby asked with exaggerated inflection. She'd always had a dramatic flair.

"Two. One for family and one for friends. I'm not much looking forward to them."

Tomby frowned. "The family thing I get, but what's wrong with being around your buds?" Apparently tired of petting Bran without result, she now futzed around with a length of rope, tying one kind of elaborate knot, undoing it, constructing another.

Mig shrugged. "Just don't like that much attention. Makes me uncomfortable."

"You better get used to it," Tomby said with a suggestive smile. "You're looking finer all the time."

"Stop it," Mig murmured. A blush rode his high cheekbones.

Bran wasn't smiling *or* blushing. His expression had clouded.

Jess observed the exchange with quiet interest. Had Tomby's compliment sparked jealousy in Bran? Nearly everything people said or did gave away something about them. That was why Jess wanted to be a psychologist.

Almost visibly, layer by layer, Tomby peeled her focus from the boys and reapplied it to the rope in her hands. She loved knots, claimed they were both mathematical and sensual. Apparently she and Bran had been experimenting with some kind of Japanese bondage thing involving knotted ropes.

Jess could see the appeal of a hot guy tied up. He just didn't want to do the tying. Mig was the one with the sharp eye and steady hand. Jess, however, felt clumsy enough to turn a rope-bondage session into a macramé class from hell. He'd probably cut off some poor dude's circulation. Then gangrene would set in, and he'd have a whole lot of explaining to do to a whole lot of displeased authority figures, not to mention a limbless ex-trick.

Tomby finally put her white rope on the coffee table, where it lay in a neat circle amid a clutter of soda cans, video games, controllers and remotes, pot paraphernalia, and sprawl of explicit yaoi and yuri manga.

"I've been trying to figure out what knot should represent us." Elbow set on knee, she rested her chin in one hand and, with the other, thoughtfully lifted and rearranged sections of the rope.

That did it. Jess got up. *No. Fuck this.* He'd be starting college as a second-semester freshman in January. He didn't want to think of himself as inextricably bound to some stupid club built on adolescent delusions.

Anxiously, Mig glanced up at him. His look was like an imploring whisper: *Don't leave me here.*

"I thought dominoes represented us," Jess said. According to Tomby, their duotone color scheme stood for XY and XX; their variety of pairing possibilities stood for sexual openness; the fact they were rectangular instead of square stood for a departure from conventional thinking and living.

The girl had quite an imagination.

"I'm not into dominoes the way I was two years ago," she said, as if she had some divine right to switch things around as she saw fit. The guys usually took the path of least resistance and indulged her.

Not anymore, Jess thought. *No matter how smart she is, she's still a kid who doesn't know* what *she wants.*

"No knots," Jess said. "Too restricting."

Tomby turned up her face and regarded him. It was a pretty face, in tones of dusky and duskier, although it still carried the pudginess of childhood. Tomby would either turn into a sultry siren or start packing on the pounds. Jess figured it could go either way.

"Then maybe you'd like *this* one," she said, putting her fingertips on the rope.

"This what?"

"Knot."

"That isn't a knot." Jess lifted the rope to reveal its dangling ends. "You had it forming a circle, and it wasn't even closed."

Tomby snatched it out of his hand and again arranged it on the coffee table. "Imagine it's an unbroken loop," she instructed him. "Which would make it an unknot or zero knot." She began crossing section over section until the rope was a jumble of overlapping curves. "Only cutting and retying it can turn it into something else. No matter how much you jag it around, it's still a loop."

"That isn't like any knot *I've* ever seen," Mig said.

"Dude. That's because it's basically a mathematical abstraction." Tomby had assumed her slightly haughty, I-know-better-than-you tone. "It only theoretically has physical properties."

Jess sighed. He was too tired to absorb the concept. "Whatever. I've gotta go." As he reached for his cell, which he'd put on the coffee table, he felt Bran's eyes on him.

Bran was shrewd. He did more observing than talking, which meant he always paid attention to what went on around him—if, that is, he thought it might affect him somehow.

"You sure you can't stay?" Bran asked, his voice smooth and low.

Uh-oh. That question meant he was hoping for some action. He and Jess hadn't done anything stupendous together—just some light kissing and mutual groping that had led to a few handjobs—but Jess wasn't in the mood tonight. Maybe the likelihood of Tomby's participation had something to do with it. And the likelihood of Mig's imminent escape.

Jess rubbed his face with his free hand. "I'm beat, man. Working at the Ren Faire is kicking my butt."

His answer seemed to be some kind of signal to Mig, who also got up. "I should go too."

Bran's pale blue eyes moved between them. "Hm. Too bad. Tomby and I had something fun planned. With ropes." He fell against the back of the couch, legs spread, and idly drew his hands up his thighs. "You sure you don't want to get in on it?"

Jess thought of being bound against Mig's smooth, hard body, and maybe against Bran's slimmer one too, and his dick stirred with interest.

Only… Mig wasn't staying. And Tomby was.

No knots. And no girls.

"Nah, I really gotta go."

"Me too," murmured Mig, shoving his hands in his pockets.

Bran stared at them a moment longer. Beneath his pot-heavy eyelids, the whites of his eyes had begun to redden. He finally dismissed his friends with a lift of the brows and an "Okay. See ya."

He clearly wasn't pleased.

CHAPTER 2

LAKE MICHIGAN'S familiar odor tinged the humid darkness. Jess gratefully drew in the smell. The Nygaards had fled Sunrise Street as soon as Mr. Nygaard's inheritance had started paying out following some lengthy legal dispute. They now owned this near-mansion on a huge corner lot just a block from the lake and amply shaded with mature trees.

Those trees rustled faintly as a water-cooled breeze cut through the sodden air. For a brief, fanciful moment, Jess imagined fish swimming among the maple leaves.

He felt relieved. Getting out of Bran's basement seemed like a kind of liberation. So Jess dawdled for a while, reveling in his freedom. As he leaned against the passenger side of the old Ford Escort he'd bought from his brother Joel, a dainty pattering that reminded him of sleet against glass drifted up from the driveway. Rust had begun to eat the Escort's shell from the bottom up, and Jess had obviously jostled the car enough to let loose a flurry of flakes.

Mig paused too, resting against the newer Toyota pickup he'd found on Craigslist. He and Jess faced each other in the dim golden glow cast by a streetlamp. Fog had begun to creep off the lake on cat paws and swaddle the lights.

The night felt imbued with strange magic—strange, because this was just another lazy summer evening in a small, quiet town, and there shouldn't have been anything magical about it.

"Feels good to be out of there," Mig said.

"Yeah, it does."

For the first time in a while, Jess noticed the tiny, scattered burns on Mig's hands. Mig had long ago dismissed them as an occupational hazard. He usually had a few charred holes in his clothing, too, but tonight he'd obviously made a point of wearing a clean, scorch-free T-shirt. It hugged his upper body in a way Jess couldn't ignore.

"I don't think I'll be coming back here," Mig said. "Not to hang out, anyway."

Jess didn't know whether to be disappointed or elated. "I don't think I will, either."

Mig's gaze, wide with surprise and glittering with lamplight, jumped to Jess's face. "Why?"

"Because that so-called 'club' is bullshit. It's always been bullshit. It has no relevance to me whatsoever."

Mig jerked out a few nods. "That's how I feel. I don't know why I let myself get sucked into it in the first place." He looked down again. "So... is that why you won't be rooming with Bran in Madison? You're trying to pull away from this crap?"

The question caught Jess off guard. True, he and Bran would both be going to UW, and true, Jess wouldn't be one of Bran's roommates, but he'd never analyzed his reasons for rejecting that option.

"I'm not sure," he said. "Maybe it's because he's starting in the fall and I'm not. Anyway, it just never occurred to me to move in with him."

"Really?"

"Yeah, really. I don't know why you find that so odd."

Mig got dodgy. He hesitated before answering. "You're friends. He likes you. Probably a lot more than he likes me or Tomby."

13

Jess felt his eyebrows pull together. "What're you getting at?"

Mig shrugged with one shoulder as he scuffed a sneakered foot against the driveway. "The two of you booking out of this burg and being roommates in college… it just seems like the perfect chance to… you know."

What the fuck? "No, I don't know."

"Start dating," Mig blurted out.

Jess couldn't stifle his disbelieving laughter. "What?"

Even through the shifting shadows cast by the trees, Mig's blush was obvious. "Don't play dumb. We all know we're not the way Tomby described."

"Why, Mr. Finch,"—with a teasing smirk, Jess crossed his ankles and his arms—"are you telling me you're a straight boy?"

"C'mon, Jess, don't fuck with me." Mig moved his sole more fitfully over the driveway's surface. "You know that ain't it."

"Yeah, I do," Jess said quietly. His amusement had drained away. "And I know I'm not straight either. Or bi. And *you* know it. At least I think you do." He paused, waiting for confirmation.

Mig pursed his lips and nodded.

I'll be dicked, Jess thought. *We just outed ourselves to each other. It's about freakin' time.* "And we both know Bran does like girls."

"The fuck. He don't like 'em as much as he likes *you*."

That was something else Jess hadn't given much thought to. Hell, it seemed he was neck-deep in denial when it came to Bran. "You really think so?" he asked.

"Yeah, I do." Mig glanced up. "What, are you deaf and blind?"

No, Jess wasn't. He'd just never wanted to acknowledge Bran's focus. Jess was actually kind of creeped out by the thought of Bran putting the make on him, but he wasn't sure why. And there was the reason for his state of denial.

14

Mig remained silent and kept his head downturned, as if he were trying to accomplish something by swiping his foot over the concrete and had to keep track of his progress.

"I'm just not interested," Jess said. He couldn't stop looking at Mig—the satiny curls of his dark hair, the short, straight line of his nose. For the first time, or maybe not the first, Jess was struck by the artistic bone structure of Mig's face, shadowed now into crests and hollows. "I mean, I'm not interested in Bran. Not in that way."

Mig's gaze flickered up. "No?"

"No."

And back down. "I don't get it."

"What's not to get?"

"He's smart, you're smart. He's good-looking, you're good-looking. And once you're in Madison, you'll have... opportunities you don't have here."

"Trust me, I don't want any opportunities. Not with him."

Was Mig being sullen or self-conscious? Was he expressing envy or just offering observations? With Mig, such distinctions weren't easy to make.

Jess had to say something fast, before Mig could resume grilling him about Bran. He quickly considered all the questions that were bouncing around in his head. "So, uh... why do you suppose it took us so long to admit the truth about ourselves?"

"I don't know," Mig said thoughtfully. "At first we were just too young, I guess. Then we all got caught up in Tomby's world of make-believe. That's all I can figure."

"I suppose that world gave us a place to fit in. And gave us hope."

Mig looked puzzled. "Fit in, yeah. Or so we thought. But hope?"

"Hope that we weren't so far gone we couldn't be 'normal' some day," Jess said, and immediately felt the sting of that

15

statement's meaning.

Mig must've felt the sting too. A slight flinch made his features contract.

At least now they were looking at each other, really communicating. Little by little, whatever self-protective impulses had stood between them were shredding and blowing away. They'd bumbled across a threshold. After all these years of limited acquaintance, they were finally coming together. Maybe for the first time in his concealment-saturated life, Jess realized, he was getting a glimpse of what true friendship was all about.

"So you're sure you're not bi?" Mig asked.

"One hundred percent positive."

"Same here."

Although Jess had suspected as much, Mig's admission still gave him a little thrill. "Have you come out to your family yet?"

Mig coughed out a single, sour laugh. "Are you kidding? Why do you think I got a job at Lancer's Metal Fab instead of working in my dad's body shop? I was afraid he'd catch me looking at some customer the wrong way."

Jess smiled. "I hear ya." He often had trouble keeping his eyes to himself. The Renaissance Faire posed a real challenge to his restraint; it was crawling with hot young men.

Mig returned a more subdued version of Jess's smile. "I'll bet you do. I've seen how you work your ass when cute guys are around."

Jess leaned forward, laughing in surprise. "Seriously? I really do that?"

"That's what it looks like to me."

"So how long have you been watching my ass?"

Mig briefly broke eye contact as another blush surfaced. "I don't know," he mumbled. "It ain't like I been marking off the days on my calendar."

The air between them seemed to thicken, but it had nothing to do with the dew point. They both shifted their positions. For Jess, it was like trying to relax inside a sleeping bag that felt too snug around his body.

"Have you scored much?" he asked, aware of a difference in his tone. It was tighter, and just a shade gruffer.

"A little. With Bran, of course. And one dude from school. And a customer who asked for Lancer's portable service 'cause he wanted to get me alone in his shop."

The revelations were casual, but they left Jess dumbfounded. If he'd had to put money on it, he would've bet Mig was still a virgin. Now it looked like Mig was more experienced than *he* was.

Bran? he'd almost barked in shock. *You got it on with Bran? Where? When? How far did you take it? And what dude from school?*

Jess tried to project an urbane attitude. He pulled down his mouth and slowly nodded, as if he took the Bran encounter for granted and didn't find the high school hookup worth inquiring about.

"How old is the customer?" he asked laconically.

"Older than us," Mig said with a taunting half-smile.

Goddamn. This was a side of him Jess had never seen before. "Are you, like, having an affair?"

"Nah. We got together a few times, and then I found out he was married."

Jess must've had *some* degree of astonishment written on his face, because as Mig watched him, he grew somber.

"Shit, who am I kidding?" he said. "I don't wanna be some older guy's twink fantasy. Or some married guy's homosexual fantasy. But mostly I don't wanna be…"

"…found out," Jess said, because he didn't want to hear Mig say, *I don't want to be this way.*

17

Mig nodded. "What about you?" he asked timorously. "The Faire is like Temptation City."

"Yeah, I've scored there. Nothing to brag about, though. Hell, it's where I work. Serious cruising would be too risky." True enough, but in addition, Jess didn't want to admit how difficult he found it to sort the gay men from the straight ones, the unattached and willing from the attached and unwilling. His difficulties were compounded by the fact that his job kept him mostly behind the scenes.

He and Mig lapsed into a stillness that was anything but static.

Knowing what to do next required no thought. Not even a split second's worth. Jess stepped forward and cradled Mig's face in his hands. He brushed his thumbs over the smoothly shaved skin, dampened by the fog, and looked into those depthless brown eyes.

"I've wanted this for so long," he whispered.

Slowly, he pressed his lips to Mig's.

Now Mig held Jess's head, held it in place as he made a thin sound that seemed trapped far down in his throat, and his lips went sensuously soft then firm then soft again as he flexed them, and his mouth opened, and his hands slid down to Jess's ass and gripped it just as their tongues made a sliding connection.

"Dylan," Jess kept whispering against and through Mig's supple, eager lips. "Dylan." He stroked Mig's hair, cupped the back of his head.

Reflexively, they pushed and ground their hips together, irresistible force meeting immovable object, until arousal flashed through Jess's body like a line of flares. He was going to come in his pants, he realized with nebulous alarm. He didn't want to, he wanted to keep kissing and feeling Mig and rubbing against his hard-on for hours, but doing those things for even ten more seconds would end it.

Panting, Jess broke the kiss and trailed his lips and tongue down Mig's throat, pulled at the neckline of Mig's shirt until it dipped below his collarbone. Jess sucked at the exposed patch of skin, hot and misted with fog and sweat, and let one hand stray to Mig's crotch. Everything was out of his control now, the sucking and biting, stroking and squeezing, and to prove it Mig grasped both sides of Jess's face and pulled it upward for their wildest kiss yet— wet and deep and careless, and dizzying as hell.

Jess's balls tightened. His muscles felt ready to spring from his skin. Mig murmured something near Jess's ear but Jess couldn't hear words, only feel a stream of fevered breath.

They pushed their stiffness-thickness-fullness together, dry humping like maniacs—Christ, the feeling!—until they were huffing into each other's pores and holding on wherever they could and those flares that ran along Jess's nerves and through his blood finally merged into a rolling wall of *oh-goddamn!*

As soon as he went rigid and began to tremble, his pelvis bucking with every clench of his ass cheeks, Mig made a guttural sound and arhythmically bucked back. Jess's legs began to quiver. He dug his fingers into whatever part of Mig's body his hands had latched on to and let the pleasure keep flowing. As soon as it began to ebb, he pushed against Mig once, twice more in a futile attempt to give his orgasm extra legs. But, inevitably, it fell away.

Panting, he and Mig rested their foreheads together. Only then did Jess realize he had Mig's biceps in a death grip, and Mig was clutching the back of his shirt.

Why the *hell* hadn't they done this sooner? And done more?

"I'm sorry," Jess managed to say on an exhalation.

Mig's soft laugh carried disbelief. "For what?"

"I think I gave you a hickey." Jess touched the spot. "Do you mind?"

"No, I don't mind. Just the opposite. I'll probably jerk off every time I look at it."

"Oh God." Another shiver of excitement shot through Jess's belly and down his legs.

"But I *am* gonna mind my dick sticking to my shorts when all the spunk dries."

Keenly aware of the cooling cream beneath the denim of his own jeans, Jess grinned. Peeling off his boxer briefs was going to be a bitch—but a worthwhile bitch.

Unsteadily, Mig eased back by a couple of inches. "God, this is weird. We've known each other for years, and all of a sudden we're jumpin' each other's bones in the Nygaards' driveway."

Oh, man, Jess thought, *don't get all abashed by it. Don't pull back now.* "I think it was inevitable," he said, hoping to allay Mig's doubts and fears—whatever their source.

"You really been wanting it?" Mig asked uncertainly.

Man, those eyes.... "Hell yes. I just didn't think *you* wanted it."

"And I thought you wanted Bran."

Jess again held the back of Mig's head, and Mig laid both hands on Jess's chest. "No. Not at all."

"Wow." Mig touched Jess's lips with his fingertips. His handsome face took on a regretful look. "Why can't this be right?"

"It *is* right. It's better than right."

"No it ain't. Isn't. Not to my family. Or this town. Not to a whole lot of people."

Jess kissed him, more gently than he'd ever kissed any guy. "Mig, we can do this. I know we can. I just wish we would've started a long time ago."

"Really?"

"Yeah. Oh yeah. And I'd like to keep going with it."

"Not in Bran's basement," Mig said, wincing a little as he tugged at the front of his jeans. "I don't wanna go nowhere in Bran's basement."

"Neither do I."

Were Bran and Tomby doing their rope thing? Jess glanced at the darkened house or, rather, at its foundation. Candlelight still wavered behind the basement windows, which were set behind shallow wells.

At that moment, he saw or could've sworn he saw the curtain move at one of them.

MIG

MOST people thought he was average distilled to its very essence, the kind and degree of average that made a person or thing virtually transparent. He'd sensed that since childhood. In school, he'd faded into the rows of desks and lockers as if they were absorbing him. On Sunrise Street, he'd been little more than a cement-colored figure rising from the pavement like a lamppost.

Being average was his greatest asset, in a way. He drew no attention, either positive or negative, which meant nobody ever felt threatened by him. Dylan "Mig" Finch—dull on the brightness scale, beige on the color wheel, easily accommodated or just as easily overlooked.

Then again, nobody had bothered getting to know him, really *know* him. Except Jesse Bonner. Blandness had never fully camouflaged him from Jess's eyes. It wasn't that Jess had poured truckloads of time and effort into debunking Mig's public image; it wasn't that Jess had shown exceptionally penetrating insight. But he'd always seemed to realize there was more to Mig than Mig was letting on. And he'd always seemed to appreciate those hidden dimensions more than the inoffensive surface that concealed them.

Other thoughts entered the eddy in Mig's mind as he scanned the bookshelves lining the left wall of his walk-in closet. The shelves represented one of those unseen dimensions. Sure, many of his peers knew he'd developed a fascination for the Vietnam War during his last year in middle school. But they didn't know why. In fact, they probably figured all he did was ogle photographs of fighter jets and Napalm-ravaged civilians. They didn't grasp his need to understand the war, a war that had led to the incision of his uncle's name on a bleak, black wall of polished marble in Washington, D.C. Even when he'd mentioned it, they still hadn't understood. Except for Jess.

In fact, few of Mig's acquaintances knew he'd always been a voracious reader with varied tastes, and those few certainly didn't grasp the "why" of that either—except maybe Jess. Although Jess had never been a withdrawn kid like Mig, he, too, must have felt different. And he did like to read. So Jess likely knew that books were often the best friends of shy boys who didn't quite fit in.

Aside from Jess Bonner, Mig's peers didn't know squat about him. They didn't even realize how inappropriate his nickname was and how he tolerated rather than embraced it. Sure, he admired the skill of VPAF and Chinese fighter regiments who'd flown MiGs in Vietnam, but he admired the MiG killers just as much—the American squadrons in their Phantoms and Crusaders. And yeah, he was a welder, but his specialty was TIG. MIG welding, just a step above stick welding, bored the shit out of him.

He ran the tip of his forefinger over spines of paper and cloth. Thank God his parents paid no attention to his books. His dad occasionally read conservative nonfiction, the kinds of ranty tracts put out by people who either worked for or made regular appearances on the Fox Propaganda Network, and his mom liked inspirational romances. By and large, though, neither one was much of a reader. They seemed to view their son's book addiction the way they'd viewed his fondness for model-building when he was younger—as a harmless activity that kept him out of trouble. Mig smiled at the thought. Little did they know that books were bigger troublemakers than a street gang. Keeping a library, even one this small, was like harboring a band of revolutionaries.

He dropped to a squat, the better to view his collection of vintage paperbacks. They sat on the lowest of the shelves he'd installed. Sci-fi, fantasy, espionage, and detective titles took up most of the space. But there was one book that had its own category. Mig reached for that misfit, its title mostly illegible due to backstrip damage, and eased it out of its slot. He'd discovered the gem in a box of old paperbacks he'd bought at a flea market.

Because I Lay with Him by Jess Westry was Mig's favorite of all his books. He loved the title and the author's name and the subject matter. He especially loved the book's suggestive but not-quite-lurid cover. In the background, streetlights glowed moodily over the colorful, smudged shapes of buildings, a hint of oily puddles in the roadway; in the foreground, two shirtless male figures stood, one slightly behind the other, both with their backs mostly turned to the reader and their heads lowered in shame. The story was about a youth fresh out of college—blond and clean cut, judging by the artwork—who gets involved with a drug-addled street hustler—dark and tousle-haired, ditto—and how the jaded guy drags the naïve guy into the depths of depravity. *His Urges Led Him to the Dormitory of Degradation*, read the cover's hook line. Inside, the text contained phrases like "long, bronzed limbs, made to strain and sweat with animalistic hungers" and "rumpled underwear, easily overlooked because of the forbidden fruit contained within."

Mig treasured the book in spite of a writing style that made him roll his eyes. Every time he read the title and the author's name, he thought of Jess Bonner, how he'd be happy to enter the Dormitory of Degradation and lie down with Jess. In fact, *Because I Lay with Him* became a poignantly romantic phrase to Mig, one to which he attached other phrases. *Because I lay with him... I've caught a glimpse of heaven.* Or *I understand what I need.* Or *I have the courage to be myself.* He realized Jess couldn't and wouldn't ever be the sum of his life—there were too many other things that mattered—but if by some chance they did end up in a true relationship, it would be the first miracle ever to grace Mig's wholly ordinary existence.

He eased into a sitting position and slowly ran a hand over the cover. "Jess," he whispered. After several lost seconds, he told himself to stay real.

Just because they were both gay, had surrendered to their "animalistic hungers," and might surrender to them again didn't mean they'd someday build a life together. He and Jess might be too different after all. And Mig would never, ever force an issue when self-respect demanded he let it go.

Not even if he was in love.

CHAPTER 3

"HEY, Brainiac, pass the popcorn." Jess's younger brother, Jared, slumped into the corner at the other end of the couch, nudged Jess's thigh with his foot.

Their father, stretched back in his giant La-Z-Boy recliner, muttered, "Try saying 'please'."

"Hey, Popcorn Pig, please pass the bowl you been hogging."

"Jared...." Their dad glanced up over his glasses.

Any one of their names, spoken in a certain way, was sufficient warning. The over-the-glasses look just gave it an extra punch.

"Come on, Jess." Jared's voice had skidded toward a whine.

Without looking at him, Jess swung the bowl in his brother's direction. He barely heard the muttered "Thanks," just like he'd barely been paying attention to the movie that was on.

He kept thinking of Mig, kept mentally rerunning their explosive encounter in the Nygaards' driveway. It shouldn't have been nagging at him—he'd impulsively surrendered to urges before—but he couldn't escape the feeling this was more than that, more than another shallow instance of wanting and getting, of having an itch and scratching it. He kept seeing Mig's eyes in the misty, light-mottled darkness. He kept feeling Mig's movements, tender and fierce and determined, against his body from head to knees. And those kisses… hell, he'd never exchanged kisses like that with anybody.

The movie apparently ended, because Jared tossed out a disparaging comment around the popcorn that filled his mouth. He clicked back to satellite and bounced up from the couch. Jess smiled at him. The kid was a fifteen-year-old smartass, but at least he brought some comic relief to the household. Even the way he looked was a form of entertainment.

A gangly dork in baggy clothes, Jared was hardly a babe magnet. All three boys in the Bonner clan had reddish hair, but Red had, appropriately, the reddest of them all. Joel's became browner the older he got, and Jess had lucked into a deep auburn with subtle copper highlights. Krazy Kid, however, looked as if a brilliant orange sunset were taking place right behind his head.

"Grab the bowl, Red," muttered their dad. As soon as Jared snatched it up and headed for the kitchen, the old man gave Jess a direct look.

It meant *Don't go anywhere; I want to talk to you.*

Fuck.

He swept off his glasses and adroitly tossed them onto the end table beside the recliner, a move he could've done in his sleep. "So…."

Jess cringed inside. A "so" from his father was invariably a lead-in to something Jess didn't want to hear.

"Who all hangs out in the Nygaards' rec room?"

Okay, where was he going with this? The possible paths were many, but there were three main roads leading to them: drugs, alcohol, and sex.

Jess flipped up his hands as they rested on his thighs. "The gang from Sunrise Street, mostly. To tell you the truth, it's getting pretty old."

"Then why do you keep going there?"

"It's something to do. I go other places too, you know."

The old man's mouth tightened. "We're getting away from my original question."

"I think that's what he wants," Jared mumbled around the granola bar clamped between his teeth. He'd just shambled back into the living room.

Jess pitched a throw pillow at him. Red deftly caught it and flung it back.

"Dad, I'm all grown up now," Jess said.

"More or less. But you're still my son."

Jared, obviously sensing a topic of interest, flopped onto the couch.

"What brought this on, anyway?" Jess asked, his irritation growing. He was in no mood to be double-teamed by his suspicious father and nosy kid brother.

The old man, who wasn't all that old, took a sip of decaf from the mug that sat on the end table. "I hear that Mexican girl spends a lot of time with Brandon."

"She isn't Mexican. She was born here. And her parents have citizenship." Jess almost added, *Shit, you know the Martinez family*, then realized it was his mother who knew them, not his father.

Mr. and Mrs. Martinez had bought their place on Sunrise Street after the Bonners' divorce, after Dad had moved to Oshkosh following a wintry stretch of looks and words so frigid they'd seared Jess's ten-year-old soul. His parents had targeted each other with those looks and words, not their sons, but the boys had felt them nonetheless.

Mom had stuck it out alone with her kids for five years, give or take, until Joel went into the military. Then, her meager reserves of patience and maternal instinct tapped out, she'd bailed. Jim Bonner had dutifully returned to Cold Harbor so Jesse and Jared wouldn't be uprooted. He'd immediately sold the House of Ugly Memories on Sunrise Street and bought a smaller place at the other end of town.

No, he'd never become acquainted with the Martinez family. But he'd obviously been hearing about their middle daughter.

Red squawked out a laugh. "Tomby? Holy crap. You know what we call her? The Balloon Man." He started snickering.

Jess whacked him in the face with a pillow. "Why don't you go play with yourself?"

"I need some magazines. But not like the ones *you* got."

The world stalled. Jess's heart felt like a rock in his chest until it slipped and plunged to his stomach. With a rare show of shame, Jared blushed, his eyelids fluttering as he looked at the pillow on his lap.

He knows. Goddamnit, the little pissbritches knows.

"Jesus Christ," the old man muttered, and it was some seconds before Jess realized their dad hadn't caught on; he was only reacting to Red's smartmouth yappiness.

"Anyway," Jess said, leaping at the opportunity to change the subject, hoping his voice didn't sound as unsteady as it felt, "why don't you just tell me what you're getting at?"

The old man sighed and pinched his fingers over his eyes. "Listen, you're a good kid. I don't want you to think I don't trust you. But I've heard about that girl...."

"S-K-A-N-K," Jared murmured, tapping the throw pillow with each letter, as if the word were printed there.

Jess wanted to glare at the kid, tell him to get lost. But he was afraid if he did, Red would retaliate by making more insinuations about Jess's secret life.

"Dad," he said, "I swear to God, whatever Tomby's up to or into has nothing to do with me. She sort of glommed onto us guys

29

when we all lived in the old neighborhood, and she never let go. We more or less put up with her. That's it."

"She's jailbait, you know," his father said.

"I realize that. And even if she wasn't—"

"She's butch," Red threw in. "She likes girls. Her and Erin Tyner are always hangin' on each other." Without another word, he bolted up from the couch and headed for his room.

In some muddled, awkward way, Red seemed to be trying to help Jess out. It might've been his way of apologizing.

"Just watch your step, okay?" the old man said wearily. "You've got too much to lose, Jesse. In fact, I wish you'd stay away from the Nygaard house altogether. I don't trust Brandon either."

Jess nodded and got up from the couch, that last declaration echoing in his mind.

Dad, endearingly clueless, kept watching him. "How's Dylan, by the way?"

Jess's world had begun to chug forward again, and now it went into overdrive. "He's… good. Doing real good."

"Nice kid. Quiet, polite, industrious."

"Yeah, he is. Just an all-around decent guy." *With an all-around nice body.*

"Hell of a welder too."

"Yup." *Really knew how to weld his lips and dick to mine.*

"I'm surprised he's not working at Tom Finch's shop."

A corner of Jess's mouth tilted up. "I guess he wants his independence. Can't stay in the nest forever."

For a moment, Jess's eyes met his father's, the same grayish green as his own, and the old man who was only forty-seven smiled in rueful understanding. Christ, how tired he looked.

He not only managed this household, he worked as an industrial designer. Because his specialty was sign painting—an outdated term, Jess thought, considering the job's reliance on computer graphics—the old man worked both at home and at the firm's headquarters in Green Bay. The office obviously had the more sophisticated technology, so Dad put in a lot of time commuting every week.

Suddenly, Jess hated the thought of leaving him, although leaving him would lessen the burden he'd borne for the past few years. So why did it feel like abandonment? Because, Jess realized, even when the old man had been in Oshkosh, he'd never let his sons down. He'd kept them fed and clothed and housed; bought them birthday cards and Christmas presents and school supplies; made sure his two weekends a month with his boys were full of family activities and the time in between was shortened by regular phone calls.

Jess stepped over to his dad's recliner and briefly squeezed the oh-so-responsible Jim Bonner's shoulders. He wasn't an extraordinary guy—not brilliant, not exciting, not even happy-go-lucky with a crackling sense of humor. But he was... there. Steady and true.

"Good night, Dad. Stop worrying about me, okay?"

The old man gave Jess's left hand two affectionate pats.

Now it was time to set a few things straight with the resident punk.

Without bothering to knock, Jess barged into Jared's room, grabbed the kid by the front of his camo-green T-shirt (which proclaimed, ironically, I DIDN'T DO IT), and flattened him against the nearest wall. Red was growing fast—was only a couple inches shorter than Jess now—but had all the muscle mass of a pole bean.

With his forefinger a millimeter from Red's nose, Jess said in a low, ominous tone, "Stay the fuck out of my room, you shit-stirring little twerp."

31

A sea of crimson buoyed Red's sparse freckles. "Hey—"

"Hey nothing. Keep your nose out of my business." Jess firmly pushed the tip of that nose for emphasis.

He remembered an observation their mother had once made while she was reading some urban fantasy novel: that Jared's freckles, when he blushed, looked like "vampire tears in a sea of blood." Jess loved his mother, but Jill Bonner was one of those in-the-Zone-alone people. She'd always been creative... and more than a little dingy.

Red was temporarily silent.

Jess released him but kept his finger in Red's face, his narrowed eyes locked onto Red's wide ones. "I'm not playin' here. Get it?"

"Okay, okay. From now on I won't go near your room, and I won't say nothin' to nobody."

Point made, Jess turned toward the door.

"FYI, dude, I don't care if you're gay."

Jess stopped in his tracks, spun around.

Red put up his hands. "Chill. I'm an enlightened guy. Live and let live and all that crap. I'm just bummed you're not the best source for dating tips."

Jess hung his head and started chuckling. Why couldn't he stay mad at this little prick?

"You okay?" Red asked warily. "You're not spazzin' out, are you?"

"No. This is just so anticlimactic."

"It's what?"

"Never mind." Jess shuffled to Jared's bed and dropped onto it. The walls in this room were like a bad acid trip, posters and artwork plastered everywhere at every imaginable angle, including sideways and upside down. Jess spotted a recent addition—a doctored picture of Justin Bieber with an arrow through his neck and a mischievous imp (that looked suspiciously like Jared) perched on the arrow's shaft. "So," Jess said, "it was the magazines that tipped you off?"

Red sat beside him. "Well, *duh*. Dongapalooza."

Elbows resting on thighs, Jess lowered his face to his hands and rubbed it. Maybe this wasn't so anticlimactic after all. The thought of his little brother paging aghast through queer skin magazines....

"You really get off on that stuff?" Red asked, suspended in a stew of disbelief, distaste, and curiosity.

Jess tilted his head and looked through his fingers. "Well, *duh*."

The kid's eyebrows went up, down. "How, um... how long have you known you're like this?"

The house seemed unusually quiet. It wasn't, of course. The old man had simply turned off the TV and gone to bed. Same drill every night.

Jess dropped his hands and loosely linked them between his knees. "As long as I can remember."

Red scraped his upper teeth over his lower lip. "What's... you know... what's that kind of stuff...?" He paused. A wince tugged at his features.

"What's it like?" Jess said with a sympathetic smile.

"Yeah."

"For me it's just right." As Jess turned a bit more to face his brother, he caught a glimpse of the custom-made T-shirt he'd ordered for Jared's twelfth birthday. *Red Rum*, it warned in jagged scarlet script. The kid had long since outgrown it, but he kept it hanging on the outside of his closet door.

"Remember your soapbox derby car?" Jess said. "The one Dad helped you build when he was still in Oshkosh?"

"Sure I do. I wanted to live in that car. We fit together perfect."

"That's what it's like."

Red looked puzzled. Then his face relaxed and he nodded.

As more questions apparently formed in his addled mind, Red nibbled the inside of his cheek. He always had to do something when he thought hard—chew a fingernail, toy with some object.

Patiently, Jess waited.

"You got, like, a boyfriend?" Red finally asked.

"No." And *bam*, just like that, Mig was in the room with them.

"D'you want one?"

Jess's stomach squirmed. "Someday."

"You gonna tell Dad you're gay? Or Mom? Or Joel?"

The squirming increased. "Someday."

Red resumed nibbling. The questions clearly weren't over. "Do you ever, like… shove stuff up your butt?"

Jess wheezed into laughter. "*What*?"

"Umfy Randall says fa—" Another blush surfaced with volcanic speed. "He says gay guys like sticking things up their butts."

Dare I ask? But it was too delicious to resist. "Such as?"

Red shrugged. "Root crops, small animals, grooming aids."

Snorting, Jess fell back onto the mattress. He lay there, both arms thrown over his face, as his laughter spiraled and his eyes spilled tears. For one thing, he didn't think Umfy Randall, who was dumber than a drumstick, was even familiar with phrases like *root crops* and *grooming aids*.

34

Abs cramping, Jess rolled onto his side and folded his legs. Oh, Christ.

"So... it ain't true?"

The kid sounded serious, which made Jess laugh even harder. "Of course it's true. If it came from Umfy Randall, it must be true." He gasped for breath and tried to control his hooting. "In fact, I'm packing a blow dryer, three parsnips, and a litter of newborn weasels as we speak."

Stony-faced, Jared regarded him. "Dude, weasels are dangerous."

Jess curled in on himself. His gut was ready to split.

If only coming out to everybody else in his life could be this much fun.

CHAPTER 4

SHIT, he missed his spare. It should've been as easy as making fun of Umfy Randall. Groaning, Jess wilted. Only one pin of the remaining three thunked onto the planks, spun a few times, and disappeared behind the wall.

That was what he got for admiring Mig's form as Mig rolled another strike on the lane to Jess's right. Damn, the guy was smooth. Jess could've watched him all day—hoisting the ball just below eye level to sight down the lane, the muscles in his forearms tightening; taking a few gliding steps to the edge of the foul line, his limbs moving in perfect concert like a dancer's; swinging that heavy bitch of a ball back and then forward and releasing it with confidence, one leg crossed behind the other just right. Yeah, Mig was a great bowler. But it was the shape and movement of his body that kept distracting Jess, not his expertise at knocking down pins.

Their relationship sure as hell was changing.

Jess shook his head in dismay as he walked back to the horseshoe-shaped bench where his five other teammates sat. Only four players participated in each game, which allowed any one of them to bow out at any time and let one of the extras step in.

There were four such teams at Crash Alley this afternoon, to accommodate the twenty-four guests at Mig's birthday party.

"Take over for me," Jess said to Shira Corwin as he dropped his sorry ass onto the bench. "I'm losing my touch." He slugged down some soda and wished it was a margarita. Plenty of the party guests had given the finger to the drinking age by sneaking in their own booze. Why hadn't *he* thought of that?

A hand slapped onto Jess's thigh and squeezed it. "You'll get it back."

That wasn't Shira's hand. Or her voice. Both belonged to Brandon, who'd slid next to Jess.

"Hm?" Jess lowered the can from his mouth.

"Your touch. I'm sure you'll get it back." Bran smiled. "You coming to my place when this bash is over? Should be about eight other people there. And some good refreshments."

"Bran, you're up!" Dalton Dagle called from the end of the lane.

"Think about it," Bran said to Jess. His smile conveyed more of an invitation than his words.

Jess fled to the men's room as soon as Bran rose from the bench.

Mig was standing at the sinks when Jess pushed the door open. Smiling, Jess clapped a hand to his shoulder. "You have a hot arm today, Boogie Boy." His eyes briefly met Mig's in the mirror before he stepped up to a urinal to take care of business.

"One of my many talents." Smiling back, Mig grabbed the lever of the towel dispenser and pumped out a few lengths of paper.

An old duffer, the only other patron in the room, pulled open the door and turned in the direction of the bar. Jess shook off... and made a decision.

Without bothering to raise his zipper and button his jeans, he lurched toward Mig, grabbed his wrist, and yanked him into one of the stalls. As soon as he'd secured the door, he freed his semi-erect dick. He lowered himself onto the toilet, moved as far back as possible, and sat cross-legged on the seat. Mig stood facing him, breath coming out faster through parted lips. He wasn't stupid enough to look befuddled or to ask what Jess was doing. He knew.

37

Jess beckoned Mig forward with a curl of his forefinger and a seductive smile. The way he was sitting put pressure on his tightening balls and made his open fly cinch the base of his cock. It hurt a little, which excited him all the more.

After Mig had stepped as close as he could, he smoothed both hands down the sides of Jess's head. Again, briefly, they looked into each other's eyes. And Jess took over.

Mouth slack, eyelids heavy, Mig watched as Jess fondled himself with one hand and traced the column in Mig's pants with the other. He made his fingers conform to that column, press firmly as they slid up and down. Mig pushed and rocked against the touch.

"Hurry," he said barely audibly, his breath hitching between syllables.

Hard to say if he was worried about other men wandering into the restroom or if he was already on the verge of letting go. Both, probably, if Jess's own reaction was any indication. Together they worked to get Mig's button and zipper undone, but it was Jess alone who worked Mig's impressive hard-on out of his briefs.

Fuckin' red briefs. What was *that* about? Jess smiled inside as he gripped the base of Mig's cock and slid his mouth down its length. That plump head passing between his lips made his own prick twitch. Mindlessly, he began stroking it.

As Mig gripped Jess's hair, Jess circled Mig's cock with his lips, cradled it with his tongue. He gave it a prolonged draw, then eased back to the tip with a series of shorter sucks as his tongue did a gliding dance along the underside ridge. Mig's hips jerked. Although there was restraint in the movement, Mig obviously couldn't keep himself from responding to the suction, to the interplay of fist and lips and tongue. So, for maybe twenty glorious seconds, he fucked Jess's mouth, the earthy musk of his arousal drifting up Jess's nostrils, the sleek, dense pole of his cock thrusting toward Jess's throat.

He came fast and hard, each contraction a distinct, deep pulse that seemed to travel straight to Jess's own prick. Excitement spangled through Jess's groin and thighs as he swallowed fast to keep up with those bolts of cream, swallowed and pumped himself and swallowed more as his balls and belly tightened and the spangles turned to sparks and his own dick throbbed in release, sharp pleasure quivering like mischievous imps through his muscles. The fluid that coated his knuckles quickly cooled against his flushed skin, and he dimly wondered how much jizz he might've splattered on Mig's clothing and his own.

Mig stood there for a moment, eyes shut and mouth open, before he eased his spent cock back into his red birthday briefs. Jess wanted to give it a goodbye pet and kiss, but he figured Mig would flinch. Jess knew how sensitive his own dick was right after he came. With a limp, lopsided smile, Mig swiped a hand down the side of Jess's face and slid the tip of his forefinger between Jess's lips. Jess gave it a half-kiss, half-suck. Mig waited several more seconds for his respiration to calm, turned around, and cracked open the stall door.

Jess was pretty sure no one else had come in—at least, he hadn't heard any telltale sounds—and Mig verified this assumption by slipping out of the stall. Water ran at one of the sinks. Jess got up, tucked his cock away and closed up shop, then flushed the toilet for show. Still weak in the knees, he left the stall.

He and Mig said nothing as they washed their hands, but an undeniable stream of feeling coursed between them, thick and sweet as syrup. Once they'd dried their hands, Jess held Mig by the shoulders.

"Happy birthday," he whispered, and gave Mig a brief but fervid kiss.

"Thanks. A lot." Cheeks rosy and dark eyes sparkling, Mig headed back to his party. Sounds rushed through the door when he swung it open—a clatter of falling pins, triumphant shouts, laughter.

Jess felt blissfully disconnected from it all. With a dreamy half-smile, he rested his hands on the sink and looked at himself in the mirror.

What's going on with you?

I like sex. Mig likes sex. It's his birthday, so I gave him a present he'd appreciate. Beats a freakin' gift certificate for an oil change, doesn't it?

Be honest.

That's the truth!

But it's not the same as being honest.

"Fuck," Jess whispered as the door opened and Paulie Schneider walked in.

"Did you just cuss at yourself in the mirror?" Paulie asked.

Jess straightened. "Yeah. I can't bowl worth a shit today."

"Try changing balls." Paulie picked a urinal and rocked back and forth a little as he freed Mr. Happy and settled into his stance.

Again, Jess smiled. *Don't need to change 'em. They'll fill back up soon enough.* "I think I just need more practice." A residual tingle teased his groin. *Mm-hm. Way more practice. I'd enjoy that.*

He decided then and there he wouldn't be going to Bran's place to get it.

AFTER a couple more hours of bowling, pizza-eating, and clandestine drinking, the party's collective energy palpably waned. People drifted up to Mig, delivered final birthday wishes, and drifted away. Some discussed where to go next, since it was only seven o'clock on a Saturday evening, and Bran Nygaard moved from one guy or girl to another, maybe reiterating his invitation to hang out at his place.

As Jess returned his rented bowling shoes, Bran appeared beside him at the counter. "Well, you coming over?" he asked, draping an arm over Jess's shoulders. The mingled odors of Bran's cologne and hair product rode the slight dampness of his clothing.

For some reason, Jess found the combination unpleasant.

"I think I'll head on home," he said, turning away from the counter and slipping out of Bran's loose embrace. "I haven't bowled in over a year. I'm already starting to ache all over."

"Maybe you could use a massage," Bran said slyly.

Jess forced a smile. "Only if there's a masseur waiting for me next to my bed."

Peering past Bran, he lifted a hand in greeting to Mr. Finch, who'd apparently arrived to settle his tab with Crash Alley. Mig stood beside his dad, and Jess couldn't help flashing him a smile.

Bran turned to see what Jess was looking at, then refocused on Jess. "Is something going on between you and Mig?"

The tone of the question—insinuating, almost accusatory— was more jarring than the question itself. Jess and Mig had only just begun to get cozy with one another, and so far, they'd been discreet.

"What do you mean, 'going on'?" Jess said, donning his clueless face. "There's nothing going on that hasn't gone on since we were kids."

Bran's mouth hooked into a smirk, and at that moment, Jess disliked him more than he ever had before. He disliked those faded blue eyes, which seemed to slice into people like chips of ice; hated that artfully colored, chopped, and gelled blond hair. Everything about Bran was sharp, from the blunt gold spikes of his eyelashes to his thin nose to his chin—and Jess suddenly found those features much too emblematic of his personality. Hell, even the knobs at either end of Bran's collarbone, visible above his scoop-necked shirt, looked like they could double as weapons.

"Anyway," Bran said, his voice sinking to a suggestive murmur, "the offer still stands. And I mean throughout the night." He moved closer by a step. "I have this craving to get down 'n' dirty with you, Mr. *Boner*. One on one."

The come-on was a hard hit, Bran's most pointed to date, and it threw Jess into turmoil. Desire swirled through his aversion. His pump had been primed by that all-too-brief encounter with Mig, and he well knew the spare bedroom off the Nygaards' rec room had a door that locked.

"I'll keep it in mind," he said, resenting the insidious power of his hormones. Jesus, how could he be enticed by a guy he'd just decided he didn't like?

"You do that." Bran's orange-juice-and-vodka-scented breath skated across Jess's face. "I've got some great toys too. I'd love to try them out with you." He leaned toward Jess's ear and whispered, "I'll make you come so fucking hard, you'll set off an earthquake in fucking China." With a final smile of promise, Bran strolled away.

Jess swallowed to moisten his dry throat. He put on his street shoes and made his way to Crash Alley's front doors, distractedly tossing out goodbyes along the way.

Outside the peppy, machine-cooled brightness of the bowling alley, the air was heavy and the sky choked with clouds. Still in a haze of confusion, Jess pulled his car keys out of his jeans pocket and unlocked the driver's door on his rust-riddled Ford.

"Hey, got any plans for tomorrow?"

The voice made Jess jump. He slumped against his vehicle as he turned.

"What's with you?" Mig asked on a chuckle.

Jess shook his head and stood up straight. "Nothing. Just lost in thought, I guess."

"Well, think about this. You want to go fishing in the morning?"

Now more confusion as Jess took in a face he *did* like, a lot, and wondered if "fishing" was a code word for less innocent activity. But Mig's guileless expression told him it wasn't. "Are your folks taking the boat out?"

Mr. and Mrs. Finch had a fairly new cuddy, a nifty, spacious craft outfitted for fishing. Only, Jess didn't want to hang out with them. Mig's parents were fine people and upstanding citizens, so wholesome they shone like polished apples, but that was precisely why Jess had never felt comfortable around them. They each seemed to wear two faces, one carefully applied over the other. Mr. Finch was magnanimous… but stern. Mrs. Finch was gracious… but judgmental. Their smiles always seemed more studied than spontaneous.

"I have no idea what their plans are," Mig said. "I just thought you and me could drown some worms off the pier. Or maybe at the Point. I had a hellacious week at work, and then I had to put up with all this party crap, so I'd like to kick back for a day."

Jess's face relaxed into a smile as he took in Mig's face, sculpted but not sharp, and more handsome by the day, and always sincere. His black hair had subtle, natural highlights, and those lush curls were trimmed just enough to keep his vision unimpaired and his appearance neat.

For all his reserve, Mig was turning into a damned striking man, and Jess's heart seemed to melt a little more each time he looked at this friend he'd once taken for granted.

"Sounds good." Jess glanced at the lowering sky. "As long as we're not in for a soaker."

"Possible thunderstorms tonight but sunny tomorrow."

"Okay." Jess impulsively ran a hand down Mig's upper arm. His skin was lightly tanned and smooth as satin. "Give me a call around nine."

Bran's invitation no longer tempted Jess. Its allure had evaporated from the warmth in Dylan Finch's eyes.

Mig

His father, who liked to brag about having raised him so well, clapped him on the back. "Well, has it been a good eighteenth birthday for you?"

Mig had just returned to what he thought of as the Dollhouse. His dad's question, and his mother's pleased smile, immediately sparked a flash of guilt. "Yeah, it's really been great. Thank you both."

His mother kissed him on the cheek. "We were more than happy to make your day special." She hadn't come to the bowling alley with Dad. Hell, she was probably still cleaning up after the birthday buffet she'd staged yesterday evening. Around twenty of Mig's relatives had showed up—aunts, uncles, cousins, grandparents—but his mother wouldn't let him lift a finger to help out. It seemed her whole life was dedicated to serving her family and the local Methodist church.

As if to prove it, she took the box of mostly gag gifts from Mig's arms and carried it toward the living room. "Let's see what you've got here," she said cheerily over her shoulder.

"Mom, you might not want to do that. Some are kind of—"

"Risqué?" his dad said with a lift of the eyebrows and a knowing smile.

"Worse."

That netted Mig not just a clap on the back but a good-natured shake, too. "Angie, maybe you'd better leave it alone," Dad called out.

Tom Finch was ex-military. He had a red-blooded appreciation for all things manly, except profanity, and might even get a kick out of the drawing Jared Bonner had sent along: a caricature of Mig— scowling ferociously, hairy all over, and bulging with muscle—in a kind of superhero Viking outfit. In one hand, he held up a roasted chunk of leg-shaped meat with a big bite torn out of it. His other hand was clamped over his crotch. The caption read, *Grrr! Now I'm a man!!!*

"So," Dad said, "I heard some scuttlebutt about Brandon Nygaard having an after-party party at his house. Didn't you want to go?"

"Nah, I'm beat. Guess I'm partied out."

"That's probably a good thing. The Nygaards need to keep closer tabs on what their kids are up to. I'd hate to see you get caught up in some mess brought on by their lax parenting."

Mig's father had little respect for Brandon's father. The two men couldn't have been more different. Tom Finch was a self-made man with a public-school education. Nels Nygaard was, according to Tom, "a trust-fund kid" with a prep-school and private-college education. The Finches were conservative churchgoers, active in the community. The Nygaards loved to travel and live the high life; Cold Harbor was little more to them than the seat of the family fortune and a place to park their asses between trips.

And as for the "lax parenting" accusation, Mig couldn't dispute it.

He had another spring of guilt... and on its heels, a hypocritical thought: Was Jess going to that party? As bad as Mig felt about the secret goings-on in Bran's basement, he wouldn't hesitate to be there if Jess was there too. But he hadn't bothered to ask.

45

Little did his father know that his favorite present of all had been a blowjob delivered by a guy in a toilet stall. That was about as manly yet unmanly as a gift could get—and, in the Finches' eyes, a bigger and fouler mess than any brought on by the Nygaards' irresponsibility.

CHAPTER 5

JUST about every person who'd been raised in Cold Harbor had had plenty of exposure to fishing, both recreational and commercial, and many residents were also familiar with a whole lot of other sports. Jess had always figured that was just the way it was in small towns. Being gay didn't give you a pass, either. If you wanted friends and a variety of ways to fill your leisure time, you went fishing and swimming in the summer, and maybe played softball or volleyball or pitched horseshoes. Then, as the weather cooled, you shot animals in the woods and fields, and shot pool in bars, and you waited with bated breath for enough snowfall to cushion your Arctic Cat or Polaris or Ski-Doo. In middle school and high school, the real stars worked football, basketball, and/or hockey into the mix.

Jess had never been a star. He'd just done what he had to do to keep himself entertained. So he fished and swam, bowled and threw darts. As he grew up, he realized he lived in a northern Mayberry— with a sordid, twenty-first century undercurrent of drug abuse, alcoholism, juvenile delinquency, and domestic violence.

And underground splinter groups like the Domino Club. Because any kind of sexual activity other than married adult heterosexual activity wasn't supposed to exist.

After Jess parked in the lot at the public boat launch, he opened the Escort's hatch, eased out his rod and reel, and lifted his modest tackle box as well as a small, soft-sided cooler. Mig was already there, sitting on the lowered gate of his truck. And damn, did he look adorable. Kind of like a grown-up Huckleberry Finn. A *hot*

Huckleberry Finn. He raised a hand in greeting and jumped down from the gate.

He wore ragged cutoffs that conformed beautifully to his ass and a lemon-yellow tank top that glowed like a sunflower against his browned skin and the fine embroidery of black hair on his chest. Those clipped curls fluffed out around the edges of his worn Milwaukee Brewers ballcap.

It was the damnedest thing, Jess thought, how he suddenly couldn't keep his eyes, or his mind, off a guy he'd known since they were grubby brats. Getting intimate with Mig had obviously thrust them both through a barrier that had risen over the years of their acquaintance, a screen that hadn't allowed them to see each other in a sexual way.

Now, Jess couldn't help but stare. He wanted to tackle Mig and shove him back into the truck, crawl on top of him and gobble him up. He cast a longing glance into the capped dimness of the truck bed and wondered if he should go for it.

Nope, too late. Mig had already begun rummaging through the gear in his vehicle.

Watching him with a bemused smile, Jess ambled up to the truck. "How the hell much crap did you bring? It's not like we're going to circumnavigate the globe to hunt whales."

Mig rolled his eyes and shook his head as he rested his fishing rod against the side of the truck. "Man, I couldn't get out of the house without somebody shoving something at me." He poked at a gargantuan, three-tiered tackle box. "My father stuck *this* in here." He lifted an insulated picnic basket. "My mother pushed *this* at me as I was walking out the door."

Jess was already laughing. "Did anybody think to send along a donkey and cart?"

"Christ," Mig muttered through a smile. He lifted a small Styrofoam bait bucket, which was probably all he planned on carrying aside from his rod and reel. Within its damp, dark confines,

48

liver-colored night crawlers curled sluggishly through their bedding of peat moss or coir.

Jess didn't have to lift the lid to know what was inside. Not only had he toted around plenty such buckets himself, but worms had always been Mig's favorite bait.

"Wait," Jess said as Mig was about to close up his truck. "Is there food in that basket?"

Mig gave him a lifted-eyebrows look. "No, Jesse, it's full of kilos. My mother's a drug runner."

"Smartass." Jess grabbed the basket. "We can't leave it here. The stuff's gonna spoil."

Mig looked indecisive. "How far are we going?" He slipped on the pair of sunglasses that hung from the neckline of his shirt... and magically looked a little older, a little hotter.

The jetty that led out to Cold Harbor Light was a favorite perch for fishermen, and today it was lined with anglers.

"Pier's pretty crowded," Jess said.

Mig gave it a look. "Yeah, let's walk to the Point."

Good thing Jess's six-pack cooler and Mig's bait box had shoulder straps. That convenience left their hands free to carry their fishing rods, the small tackle box, and the eats.

They followed the paved path that led from the parking lot to Driftwood Point. It wasn't crazy crowded, but at least a half-dozen bicyclists and skateboarders flew past the strolling pedestrians. Locals mixed with weekenders. The latter far outnumbered the former.

Erin Tyner, one of Tomby's pals, lifted a hand as she sailed past on a pair of inline skates. She had lank hair colored like black and cherry licorice and wore makeup to match. Jess barely knew Erin, since she hadn't been in his class, but she had a sneering, swaggering air that always made him think of the movie *The Lost Boys.*

Mig acknowledged her by uncurling two fingers from the handle of the basket he carried. Jess saluted with his fishing rod.

"My kid brother claims she's 'butch'," Jess said. "She's supposedly pretty tight with Tomby."

Mig pondered this. "Hard to say. Seems to be a whole group of girls who don't know what they are. Or like pretending they're something they're not."

"Which reminds me, why wasn't Tomby at your party yesterday?"

"I didn't invite her."

"But why?"

"Mostly because the people who were there don't really know her, and she doesn't know them."

Jess studied Mig's face, which remained impassive. "Why do I have a feeling there's more to it than that?"

They walked several steps before Mig answered. "'Cause maybe there is. Maybe I want to pull away from that Domino Club crap and start acting like a big boy who knows what he wants."

Instead of being some meek follower who's afraid to admit what he wants. Yeah, Jess understood. It gave him an unexpected thrill to hear that proclamation, and another small jolt as he realized just how quickly, with how little fanfare, Mig Finch was becoming a man. A lot of their male peers liked to strut and crow and engage in all kinds of reckless behavior to prove their maturity—Jess thought some of them would wear their nuts around their necks if they could—but Mig wasn't like that at all. He'd obviously been growing his stones quietly, in private, and didn't feel a need to prove any-goddamned-thing to any-goddamned-body.

"Think you'll ever hook up with Bran again?" Jess asked. Much to his chagrin, he'd felt a tad insecure—and maybe jealous or envious; he couldn't determine which—since Mig's confession. The feelings nibbled at him like minnows. He wanted to banish them.

Mig slid him a glance and a smile. "Not anymore. It was just one of those what-the-hell things anyway. Spur of the moment."

"Was it good?"

"Only good enough to do the trick. Didn't mean nothin'. I mean, anything."

"Mig, you don't have to keep correcting yourself," Jess said gently.

"Yes I do. One of the best pieces of advice I ever got from my father was, 'Life is a never-ending process of self-correction.' I can't let myself forget that."

Jess nodded, then started chuckling.

"What? You don't think it makes sense?"

"Sure I do. It makes perfect sense. But I just remembered a piece of advice I got from my little brother."

"You're kidding me. Red Rum gives advice?"

"You bet."

Now Mig was grinning. "What was it? 'Don't use your underwear as a slingshot for dog poop'?"

Jess's head fell forward as he laughed. The kid had actually done that. Or tried. "No. It was, 'Weasels are dangerous.'"

Mig looked utterly mystified.

Jess kept snickering. "I'll tell you about it later."

HANGING out at the lakeshore proved a surprisingly pleasant way to spend that Sunday afternoon. Jess couldn't have asked for more. Unless, of course, there'd been a hut on Driftwood Point reserved for him and Mig, and it contained a bed and had a sturdy, locking door.

They caught and released maybe a dozen young perch and a

good-sized smallmouth bass, munched hardboiled eggs and smoked salmon on crackers, sipped beer. Other people wandered onto the Point, hung out for a little while, and wandered away again. A clutch of drunks in an older deckboat tried mooring there but couldn't manage it; Driftwood Point had no dock.

Jess recounted his pivotal conversation with his kid brother. When Mig asked if other people's names had come up, and he obviously meant his own, Jess said no. He'd come out to Red because he hadn't had much choice. It seemed to have turned out well, and the kid had promised to keep his lips zipped.

"You're lucky," Mig said. "Your family's pretty awesome. I figure if I ever come out—"

"If you ever?"

"Okay, *when* I come out, no matter how it happens, my parents ain't gonna see me the same." Mig shook his head decisively. "No way. I don't know if we'll be able to work through it or not, but even if they don't disown me, we'll probably act like stick people around each other."

Jess briefly put an arm around Mig's back.

After a few hours of casting off the rocky shoreline, they moved to the shady patch of grass where they'd set the picnic basket and cooler. The grass had already begun to dry after last night's rain. Mig reclined, took off his sunglasses, and pulled the bill of his cap farther over his eyes. Jess sat beside him and cracked open another beer. He lifted the sunglasses off Mig's chest and slipped them on, because he'd neglected to grab his own pair off the dashboard.

"Don't," Mig said, touching Jess's arm. "You don't need them, do you? The sun's behind us."

"You afraid of germs?" True, Jess could've used the glasses earlier rather than now, but he found Mig's request strange. Mig never refused to share anything with anybody.

"I just like looking at your eyes, that's all."

Those little insect feet, the ones that had been plaguing Jess since he started getting closer to Mig, again pattered across the lining of his stomach.

"Fuck, that sounded weird," Mig mumbled as he cupped a hand over his face. "Sorry."

"You don't have to apologize."

Mig blew out a breath. "Then you might as well know that your Ren Faire outfit really turns me on too."

"Seriously?"

"Oh yeah. When I saw you in it, I wanted to feel up your ass and lick your chest."

Even when Jess worked on weekends, he still had to do chores that could get him grungy fast. So his garb usually consisted of pliable leather boots, leather chaps over thin, snug trousers, and a leather vest over a blousy shirt, which he kept open midway to his navel. It was an attempt to stay cool, not an attempt to make guys hot, but the effect of the whole ensemble had occasionally netted him more than passing attention.

Knowing how it had affected Mig made his dick start to stiffen.

Jess slipped off the glasses, laid them on Mig's chest, and skimmed a finger over the dusky expanse of skin above that bright tank top.

"You better not do shit like that," Mig murmured, his voice thick.

"Fuck," Jess whispered.

This was insane. Now they were both getting excited, and all it had taken was a reference to a costume and the briefest lustful touch. Jess wondered if that hickey was still visible... then wondered if Mig had indeed beat off whenever he'd looked at it... then got more excited. There was noticeably less space behind his zipper.

Mig bent his legs, planting his feet on the grass, and did a quick pull at the crotch of his cutoffs. The only other people at the

Point were a young couple sitting at one of the picnic tables, but they had a pretty good vantage point if they chose to watch the two male friends.

"So," Jess said, veering into safer conversational territory, "what's your fantasy vision of your future?" He looked down at Mig and spoke softly, although the other couple wasn't close enough to eavesdrop.

Mig linked his hands over his ribcage. "To claim my life, I guess. Make something of it that I *want* to make of it."

"Which is?"

"Be Dylan Finch, a good man and good welder, not Mig Finch, Tom and Angie's bashful, uptight kid. Get my own place, spend time with people whose company I enjoy. No more lying or hiding or playing games."

It was rare to hear such restrained ardor in Mig's voice. His wish, and the fervency of it, spoke to Jess's own nebulous dreams. He wondered if they'd bother making room for each other in their futures or if their relationship had slipped into its own restrictive slot—the one for short-term sexual flings.

Heavy stuff, and it immediately began to weigh on Jess. He tried for a lighter mood. "So you don't want to keep doing what we did at Crash Alley?"

"Oh, I want to keep doing *that*," Mig said with a grin as he cast Jess a look from the shadow of his cap. Just as Jess smiled back, Mig's grin faded. "Just not in toilet stalls and front seats and back rooms."

Jess nodded. Mig had inadvertently weighted their conversation even further.

It hurt to hear him talk like this. The tone of his voice hurt and the truth of his words hurt. That nagging fear of being "caught," of being found out, was always with Jess too. But his fear would soon diminish. There'd be little threat of censure in liberal Madison, and no lack of privacy.

54

Jess wanted that freedom here and now. He wanted to trace Mig's profile, run a finger over his lips, lie half on top of him and give him a deep, leisurely kiss. He hated that he couldn't do any of those things. Yet if he or Mig were female, the people who shared this little spit of land with them wouldn't mind witnessing such displays of affection. They'd even think, *Isn't that sweet?* Or *Don't they make a cute couple?*

Suddenly, Jess hated that double standard with a ferocity he'd never felt before. And it was because, he realized, he'd never been in public with a guy who'd meant something to him. Until now.

A soft creaking and rustling came from behind him. Jess glanced over his shoulder. The couple had risen from the picnic table and now strolled back toward the path.

"We're alone," Jess said.

"But we won't be alone for long." Sighing, Mig linked his hands behind his head. "Shit, Jess, just to be able to make love on a bed or even on a couch or in the shower...."

Another tingle crept through Jess's groin. "Kitchen table. Counters. Deck."

Mig smiled. "Rooftop."

"Naked to the world."

"The universe!" Mig thrust a hand toward the sky, fingers outspread.

Without thinking, Jess reached up and laced his fingers through Mig's. Together, they slowly lowered their hands to the strip of trampled grass between their bodies. Mig squeezed Jess's hand, and Jess lifted Mig's and kissed it.

"I like your vision," Jess said quietly.

Voices sounded at their backs. Reflexively, they disengaged their fingers.

Jess rested his arms on his upraised knees. "Where are you going to find all the guys to populate this fantasy?"

Mig gazed at the quaking crown of leaves overhead. "One would be enough to make me happy. The right one." He sat up, repositioned his cap, and squinted at the lake as if an array of men frolicked over the glinting surface. "I just have to find him."

Another throwaway observation that caught Jess unaware and walloped him. Yeah, he had his own dreams, restless but repressed, and even if Mig only spoke Mandarin, he'd be speaking to those dreams.

Or maybe, just maybe, he embodied them.

CHAPTER 6

AFTER stashing his rod and reel and empty cooler in the attached garage, Jess entered the house. He felt restive and preoccupied. Light filled the short hallway that led into the kitchen.

Red stood at the center island, tapping what was likely some disjointed, moronic text message into his phone.

"Catch anything?" he asked without looking up.

"Yup."

"Can it be cured with antibiotics?" Grinning, Red tossed his head back. "Heh. I slay me." He proceeded to stuff nachos into his mouth from a plate in front of him. Freakin' kid was always eating yet never put on a pound.

"Why don't you steal a car and drive to Alaska?" Jess poured a glass of water and gulped it down. He'd only had three cans of beer, but once he stopped drinking alcohol, he always got thirsty as hell.

He filled up the plastic tumbler again and, as he sipped, poked idly through the three open boxes sitting at one end of the island. Every two weeks to a month, Dad religiously shipped three care packages to Joel in Afghanistan. Jess always contributed, and Jared never failed to come up with something lame and laugh-worthy. Neighbors occasionally pitched in too. Dad tried to keep the weight of each box at ten pounds or less—a limit not easy to respect when all the personal hygiene products and bundles of boot socks, the paperback thrillers and snack foods started piling up.

Jess lifted a tissue-swaddled form from one box and carefully peeled away the layers of paper. Frowning, he stared. The mystery gift was a length of vacuum-sealed jerky decked out in doll accessories, including an improvised wig, sunglasses, a bikini, and tiny high-heeled shoes. The thing looked like an anorexic woman who'd spent days in the withering glare of the sun.

"Did you do this?" he asked Red, and immediately realized what a thoroughly stupid question that was.

Red slapped on his toothiest Mr. Potato Head grin. "D'ya like it? I call it 'Beefy Barbie Goes to the Beach'."

"You have way too much time on your hands," Jess muttered as he rewrapped the piece.

Red continued to watch him. "So, is the Migster gonna be your baby-daddy?"

"Shut up, dipshit." Jess tossed the cup into the sink. He'd had a nice day, so why did he feel so out of sorts? "Where's Dad?"

"Out partying. But not like a rock star." Red made a face at whatever message had appeared on his phone. He finally shut the damned thing off and looked up, although he still leaned on the butcher-block surface of the island, clutching his link to La La Land and picking at tortilla chips slathered in coagulated cheese. "The Dembrowskis are having a cookout or something. I think they're trying to find him a squeeze."

"Like who?" Now *that* was a bulletin. The old man hadn't dated since breaking up with his girlfriend Lisa on New Year's Eve.

Red shrugged. "Whoever's desperate enough, probably." He smirked as he stood up. "*There's* a good reason for coming out. Nobody'll try to fix you up with some coke whore who has a bunch of rug rats that need supporting."

Jess shook his head and left the kitchen.

"Hey," Red shouted, "Brandon called for you."

That was more of an attention-getter than the old man being on the prowl. Jess turned and came back to the kitchen. "He called on the land line?"

"Yeah. Said you weren't answering your cell."

"That's because I left it in my car." Jess pulled his phone out of his pocket and checked for messages or missed calls. Sure as shit....

"Did he leave you anything?" Red asked.

"Nope." But Bran *had* called. Twice. Jess felt more than mere curiosity about that, and the feeling wasn't a good one. "What did he say?"

"Just wanted to know where you were and when you'd be back. Didn't sound like anything important."

Certainly not important to Red, and probably not important to Jess, but apparently important to Brandon. "And you told him?"

"Well... yeah. I got *some* manners, y'know."

This was one of those rare occasions when Jess wished his brother had been the rude little numbskull he so often was. "Thanks," Jess muttered, and again headed for the bathroom.

"You caught up in a love triangle or something?" Red called after him.

Although Jess heard the humor in Red's voice, he didn't feel it. "Your skinny ass is gonna be caught on one of my boots if you don't start watching your mouth."

Jess tuned out the kid's response as he closed the bathroom door. He was even more bothered now. As he stepped under the shower, his thoughts tumbled in the cascade of water.

"One would be enough to make me happy. I just have to find him."

"I've got some great toys too. I'll make you come so fucking hard, you'll set off an earthquake in fucking China."

Up until that spontaneous breakthrough encounter with Mig,

59

Jess had known what he wanted, at least in the short term. His desires had been simple ones: earn as much money as possible and, the rest of the time, squeeze in some fun. He'd expected that fun to take the form of casual partying—some drinks here and there, some pot, lots of laughs, and maybe an occasional handjob if he couldn't find the right guy and the right place to take things further.

Actually, "taking things further" hadn't been that much of a concern. There was always the Internet. Jess could safely and comfortably cruise the Net in the privacy of his room if he ever craved more spice with a bigger kick. Alone with his handy-dandy dick sleeve and images of bad boys doing naughty things, he was assured of finding enough excitement to keep him content.

Only… everything was different now. Jess's interest in partying had dwindled as his interest in Mig had grown. Simultaneously, Bran's promises of earth-shaking orgasms threatened to eclipse the meager satisfaction of masturbation as well as the emotional high of being with Mig.

As Jess soaped his body, his right hand frequently detoured to pull and stroke his dick. But he had trouble focusing on a single fantasy. Wanton anonymous boys merged with Mig's face and body and kisses; all the hurried play with Mig slid into visions of more prolonged play with Bran. Jess finally jumbled all his fantasies together until he managed to rub off, but it didn't feel as good as it could have. His climax seemed lacking somehow, a desperate shot in the dark with no clear target.

Goddamn, he didn't know what the hell he wanted. Why did sexual hunger have to complicate otherwise simple issues? Why couldn't *I like; I don't like* or *I need; I don't need* be enough?

A little more relaxed, at least physically, Jess went to his room and closed the door. As he slipped on a pair of pajama bottoms, he vaguely wondered if his father, even at the overripe age of forty-seven, struggled with this kind of crap. And what about Joel? He was only twenty-two. Although he likely hadn't been in a similar quandary since his deployment to Afghanistan—Christ knew he had greater horrors to worry about—he must've done *some* fretting over his love life when he was still at home.

Abruptly, Jess missed having his older brother to talk to. Even though Joel was a macho guy, he had both common sense and sensitivity.

Jess mentally offered up a quick prayer for Joel's safety as he grabbed *The Hitchhiker's Guide to the Galaxy* off his nightstand and flopped into bed. "Quit being so goddamned self-centered," he murmured. Joel continually faced the threat of gunfire and IEDs. Such danger put Jess's concerns on a par with Red's. And that was about as petty as petty could get.

Within several minutes, Jess's eyes were moving over the text without absorbing it. The old man was home—his and Red's voices floated, an unintelligible cloud of sound, from the living room—and Jess's thoughts veered in new directions.

Had Dad met someone he liked enough to ask out? Could *he* be gay? No, that didn't seem even remotely possible. So when should they have The Big Talk? Before or after Jess went off to college?

His iPhone signaled incoming.

It was a video. The sender seemed to be pointing his phone's camera at a TV set. Intrigued, Jess held the screen closer to his face.

Two naked men standing at a pool table, not a woman in sight. No, three naked men, one lying *on* the pool table. After some nipple-pinching and genital-groping, one of the standing dudes, a bearish guy, slid something up the ass of the other standing dude and wiggled it around. Jess immediately thought of Umfy Randall's bit of wisdom and was tempted to laugh—until he noticed what an exceptional ass had just received the plug, and saw the ass's owner drop his head back and close his eyes as if he'd just been swept into anal nirvana.

The bear then climbed onto the pool table and straddled the head of the reclining man, whose legs went up to accommodate the stiff rod of Plug Dude. At first Jess thought, *Ouch*, because having one's sacroiliac braced against the edge of a pool table must've been nine notches beyond uncomfortable. But... Reclining Man was being tea-bagged by Bear and fucked by Plug Dude, and there was a whole lot of shakin' (and thrusting and writhing and cock-yanking) goin' on, and all three players looked pretty damned transported by it.

Although Jess was a little tired, he wasn't paralyzed. The sights and sounds of that pool-table orgy began to get to him. Soon he was several notches beyond uncomfortable himself.

As Jess swallowed to ease his parched throat, the camera made a sweep away from the TV screen. It refocused on a real live cock being coaxed by a real live hand. Jess immediately recognized the mat of strawberry-blond pubic hair, and he didn't need any clues as to what was going on.

The screen on his phone went blank. He disconnected. Within seconds the phone buzzed again, and a text message appeared.

come & get some. then cum again. □

His dick getting chubby within his boxer briefs and his nuts starting to clench, Jess got off the bed and threw on some clothes. He didn't think at all, just let himself be led by his hunger.

Before he left his room, he sent Bran a text message: *be there in 10.*

"Where you goin'?" Red asked as Jess wheeled into the kitchen. The kid was standing in front of the open refrigerator. "Dad's home. He already went to bed. Alone."

"I gotta get something. I'll be right back."

He had to get something, all right. Checking his pockets one last time for his phone, keys, and condom packet, Jess strode down the hallway to the garage.

Somewhere in the depths of his lust-muddied brain, he concluded that certain impulses required no analysis. They simply demanded to be followed.

CHAPTER 7

IN SIX and a half minutes, Jess was parked in the Nygaards' driveway. He went straight to the basement's outside door. Once again Bran's parents didn't appear to be home. Either they were out of town or at some dinner party. Maybe they'd even deigned to go to that cookout at the Dembrowskis' place, although that wasn't likely. They moved in snootier circles.

The door was unlocked, as Jess had expected. He descended to the basement on swift, light feet. Although the stairwell was illuminated, the rec room was dark. Jess paused. A thin slice of light crept from beneath a door on the right, the door to the starkly furnished bedroom.

His pulse raced, driven by equal measures of dumb excitement and unsettling awareness. The awareness seemed to be gaining ground. As juiced up as that video and Bran's accompanying stroke-fest had made him, Jess couldn't ignore either his doubts or his simmering distaste. He didn't really want to be here, poised to do something he'd regret immediately afterward. Yet the pressure in his groin was demanding he take action.

He walked to the bedroom door and cracked it open.

Another video was on, a different one, but it had all the raunch factor of the first and possibly more. Jess glimpsed a buff young man wearing a collar and leash, heard grunts and snarled words, the smack of something against flesh, a startled cry of pleasure-pain. He looked at the bed. Bran lounged naked atop the covers, idly playing with himself, steeped in obscene cunning.

"I knew you'd give in," he said, his voice thick in tone and thin on breath. He got up, his long, slender cock angled away from his body like an arrow, and walked up to Jess. "With the right persuasion."

Another half-step, and Bran's naked body was pressed along the length of Jess's clothed one. Bran rocked his hips, sawing his hard-on against the limb in Jess's pants, and gave Jess a sloppy, enthusiastic kiss.

"I really fuckin' want you," he murmured against Jess's mouth as he pushed and pushed, the sliding pressure making Jess crazy. They were holding each other now, and Jess swept his hands down to Bran's ass and clutched it. His breaths came out hard, each one tagged with a helpless whimper. He needed to come.

"Don't ever do this to me again, Jess." Bran felt up Jess's chest beneath his T-shirt, nudged his nipples. "You just about made me beg. And I don't like begging for anything." Bran groped at the front of Jess's waist, popped the button on his jeans, lowered his zipper. "Now lose the clothes and fuck me. I'm really stoked and I need some dick up my ass."

His body was smooth and slender as a reed flute, only it was Jess who was being played, not Bran. Although Jess dimly realized this, it didn't matter now. Things had already gone too far.

Bran pulled something off the nightstand and tossed it toward the end of the bed, then climbed onto the mattress. He knelt there on all fours, offering his ass, waiting. In a fumbling rush, Jess grabbed the condom out of his pocket and slid his jeans and underwear down his legs. He couldn't be bothered removing his sneakers and socks or even his shirt.

He ignored the thing Bran had tossed his way. It was a butt plug, still in its package, but Jess had never used one before—on himself or anybody else. Hell, he'd never fucked anybody either, for that matter, or been fucked. So he'd have trouble enough just keeping his wits about him and making sure he didn't hurt Bran.

With moans and groans and occasional yelps still pouring out of the TV at his back, Jess ripped open the condom packet. He'd just begun rolling the rubber onto his bone when the bedroom door clicked open.

In heart-stopping shock, Jess jerked his head to the right. Neither Mr. nor Mrs. Nygaard loomed in the doorway. And it wasn't Tomby staring at him as he stood frozen behind Bran, who'd sunk to an awkward sprawl on the rumpled bedding. It was Mig… and the look on his face was a look Jess never wanted to see again.

"I-I'm sorry," he said with effort, his mouth barely moving when he spoke. "I didn't know…."

He took an unsteady step backward then moved out of sight.

"Hey, you don't have to leave," Bran called out. "The more the merrier." His voice was lethargic, but it carried an undertone that disturbed and angered Jess.

Amusement, that was what it was. A wry and thoroughly callous amusement.

Jess hurriedly peeled off the condom and tossed it into a wastebasket beside the nightstand. As Mig's footsteps receded up the stairs, Jess felt increasingly frantic. He bent over and pulled up his underwear and jeans, wrestling them over his erection, wincing as they hugged his aching balls.

"Where you going?" Bran asked. He was sitting up now, and he made a grab for the hem of Jess's shirt.

Jess pulled away from him. "Leave me alone."

"What's wrong with you, man? Mig's just embarrassed. He'll get over it."

"Why was he here?" Jess asked tightly. He felt his pockets to make sure his keys and phone hadn't fallen out. When Bran didn't answer, Jess spun toward him. "Why the fuck was he here, Bran?" His voice burst out of his throat as if he'd been keeping it caged there.

Bran gave a careless shrug. "I called him 'cause I have

something to give him. I didn't think he'd show up while—"

"Fucker," Jess muttered. He dashed out of the room and sprinted up the stairs, taking two at a time.

The street was quiet, which reminded Jess of something else he should do. He pulled his phone out of his pocket and set it to mute. Bran sure as shit wasn't happy about being left in the lurch, and a bitchy call was inevitable.

Jess practically dove into his car, then backed out of the driveway with such reckless speed he nearly ended up on the lawn across the street. After getting the Ford pointed in the right direction, he headed for Birch Bark Lane. Like the Nygaards and the Bonners, the Finches no longer lived on Sunrise Street—not since Tom Finch's body shop had started bringing in enough money to let him build his own house in a Cold Harbor subdivision.

After seemingly endless minutes of gripping the steering wheel and staring down darkened streets and having no idea what, exactly, he was doing, Jess pulled into the Finches' driveway. Mig's truck was there, thank God.

Jess jogged up to the front door and knocked. He didn't want to ring the bell because the Finches might've already gone to bed. Squeezing his eyes shut, he thought, *Please answer. Please.*

Mig did pull the door open, rather abruptly. He must've arrived just a few minutes before, and he likely didn't want the rest of the family disturbed by this late visitor.

"Please let me in or come out here," Jess muttered. "I need to talk to you." He stood there like a lightning-struck tree, shaken to his core, blasted by feelings he'd never experienced before: humiliation, a need to explain his behavior, a fear of losing something important to him. He tried to calm his breathing.

Tom Finch's voice boomed from somewhere upstairs. "Dylan, is somebody here?"

"It's only Jess Bonner," Mig called up the stairway. "He stopped by for a few minutes. We'll be quiet." When Mig again turned toward Jess, his face and voice were expressionless. "You should leave."

Jess shook his head and mouthed *no*.

After casting another glance up the stairs, Mig motioned Jess inside, then led him down the central hallway, through the patchy gloom of the kitchen, and out onto the patio. He sat at the large table stationed there, in the dense shadow of an umbrella open to the sunless sky. Jess, mentally cursing the pain in his nuts, sat in the chair beside Mig's.

"Why are you here?" Mig asked quietly. "We both have to work tomorrow."

Why indeed? Jess had never been as confounded by his motives as he was at that moment. It was the earlier look on Mig's face that had brought him here, the dismal slackening of those features Jess had come to adore and the responsive plunge of his spirit.

"Why did you show up at Bran's place?" he asked.

Mig stiffened. "Don't worry; I wasn't trying to muscle in on your action."

"No, that's not what I meant." For an exasperated moment, Jess dropped his head to his hands, spearing eight fingers into his hair. God *damn* it, if only that fist in his sac would relax. "Something's wrong here."

Mig chuffed out an arid laugh.

Resting his forearms to the table, Jess leaned toward Mig. "Listen to me. Remember what you said about *your* hookups with Bran? How meaningless they were?"

The glimmer of Mig's eyes disappeared as he looked down. "You don't have to explain nothin' to me. I know how it is."

"No, you don't. And I don't either. So please tell me why you were there so I can try to make some sense of this. I don't trust coincidences."

Mig sighed. "Bran called and said his parents were getting rid of a bunch of books, and if I wanted to check them out before they either hit the trash or went to Goodwill, I should come right over."

"Did he say he'd asked me over too?"

Mig's gaze flickered up, then down. "No."

"Bran never told me you'd be stopping by, either. He never said a word. He… he sort of lured me over, and when I got there he was in the bedroom, already undressed, and… shit just happened." Jess swallowed. What the fuck? He felt shame and desperation, and the feelings utterly baffled him.

Mig pursed his lips and nodded. He cleared his throat before he spoke. "You know what? I think we need to stop seeing each other. I mean, spending time alone together the way we been doing. It's just… it's maybe not good for us. And you'll be going to Madison soon."

Words spun through Jess's head, things he would've said if they hadn't tripped at every turn on his reservations. *You're the only one I want. This can't end; it just got started. We have until January. And after that, we'll be able to spend weekends together, and holiday breaks. A few hours on 151 and I'll be here. Or you'll be there. I know we can make this work. I want you, Dylan Finch.*

He couldn't say all that shit. It seemed like too much too soon. And even if it wasn't, what if he couldn't live up to those declarations? He'd certainly proved himself a fickle prick so far, hadn't he?

"You really don't want to get together anymore?" Jess sounded pathetic, probably looked pathetic too, but he couldn't have dug up a brave or carefree face to wear if he'd been carrying one in his pocket.

Mig made some indecisive movements with his head and upper body. "Well, you know, we'll just slide back to being buddies. No muss, no fuss, no bother. It ain't like we can actually go anywhere with this, make anything of it."

"Why not?" Jess whispered. He felt his face gather around the question—forehead furrowing, mouth compressing.

"Come on, you know why." Without looking at him, Mig got up. "It's getting late. I gotta hit the sack."

"Mig...."

"Just let it go, Jess. Okay? Let it go."

MIG

NO BIG deal. It ain't like we're boyfriends who went to prom together.

Mig tried to amuse himself with that image as he stared at the parallelogram of light on his bedroom ceiling. Only, the image wasn't all that funny. The two of them nearly the same height, dressed in tuxes, looking like magazine models—at least Jess looking like a magazine model—and wearing matching red boutonnières.

"Damn it," Mig whispered, slapping a hand to his forehead. What he really should put his mind to was dreaming up a reason for Jess's visit tonight. One of his parents would undoubtedly ask about it in the morning.

Jess couldn't find... something, his wallet or phone or sunglasses. He wondered if he'd left it in the picnic basket.

Yeah, that should work.

Mig flipped onto his side.

"Shit, why Bran?" he murmured to the wall. Supposedly, neither he nor Jess wanted to go back there. Not for anything like *that*. They'd both said so. They were determined to make a break from anything and everything having to do with the Domino Club.

Then he thought about what Tomby had said, that they were all part of some circle she called a zero knot, and no matter how its shape was altered, which maybe meant no matter what turns their lives took and who paired up with whom or which of them tried to avoid the others, they were still strung along this loop, bound together. The only way to change that was to break the connection, and the only way to break the connection was to cut the cord. A severed loop was no longer a zero knot.

Mig's head began to hurt.

Stop it. Her bullshit has nothing to do with anything. Just give yourself a little cool-off time, then either nudge Jess out of your life along with Bran and Tomby or go back to being casual pals with him. 'Cause this just ain't worth losing sleep over. Remember, he'll be gone in January.

It was hard, though, trying to shake that image of Jess standing behind Bran. Worse yet, Mig couldn't get over the soft explosion of pleasure he'd felt in the Nygaards' driveway, when Jess had held his face and spoken his name between kisses. *"Dylan. Dylan."*

If he could just dig those two memories out of his brain and flush them, he'd be okay. Maybe he could hasten the process by finding some action of his own.

Bastard.

Nah, Jess wasn't a bastard. He was just an O-chaser. *I've been one too.* Then Mig reminded himself he needed some sleep.

He flipped onto his other side and envisioned the best welds he'd ever executed, some so beautiful in their precision they resembled the silvered fossils of sea creatures or delicate, symmetrical ripples of gleaming sand.

Yeah, he was good. At least in that, he was damn good. No employer with sound judgment would ever favor another welder over him.

CHAPTER 8

ALTHOUGH the Great North Faire was only open to the public on weekends, Jess did most of his work there during the week. He wasn't a vendor or actor or street performer. He was a grunt.

Having a lowly position suited him just fine. He didn't have to deal with the crowds or garb up in some elaborate, sweat-inducing costume. Better yet, the nature of his labor not only kept him in shape but helped build his body.

Jess mucked out horse stalls and goat pens and laid down clean straw. If need be, he fed and watered the animals too. He helped with grounds keeping and structure maintenance as well as routine cleanup.

When he did have to work on a weekend, he both dreaded and looked forward to the change. The Faire had a noisy exuberance that made for a good time, but only in small doses. Jugglers, fools, magicians, and minstrels roamed the grounds, entertaining visitors. Pirates menaced them. Vendors hawked crafts and flowers, food and wine and ale. There were short plays in the modest amphitheater, jousting and fencing exhibitions on a beaten patch of ground called the Tournament Field. All around, banners and pennants and tent walls snapped in the breeze, and the sound of human voices mingled with the airy music of flutes, lutes, and bells.

Better than all this merriment, though, was the eye candy. Plenty of fine-looking men worked at or visited the Great North Faire. Such scenery was pretty sparse around Cold Harbor, so Jess took it in with relish.

Just in case someone made an offer he couldn't refuse, he always carried condoms in his wallet. He'd already scored twice, both times with delectable guys looking for some quick, quiet action.

This week, however, Jess didn't give a rip-roaring rat's ass about any of it. Because of Mig, damn it. All because of Mig.

Jess felt like shit. He felt like shit when he was at work and felt like even worse shit when he was at home. Nothing interested him—not the threadbare denim stretching over his coworker Seth Maloney's impressive package, not the angular bulge of some faux-knight's thighs and calves as he rode his steed during a rehearsal. Neither could Jess concentrate on video games or books or movies. Even Red's babble didn't brighten his mood. A letter came from Joel, which made him feel a little better for a little while, but its buoying effect didn't last. Hours after reading it, Jess sank again.

Day after day passed without a call from Bran. Jess found any departure from expected behavior unnerving. He'd have felt the same if his dad went on a bender or Red became as introspective as a Buddhist monk. The unease triggered by Bran's silence only compounded his distraction.

Worse yet, Jess had called Mig on Wednesday evening, but Mig had cut him off after less than a minute of self-conscious small talk.

Shifts were taking place, as if the earth had become unsettled far beneath its surface, and Jess's world suddenly seemed out of balance. Like a primitive tribesman with no knowledge of geology, he didn't fully understand why… and didn't know how to restore his peace of mind.

The week crawled by beneath the scorching glare of the August sun. Jess spent much of his time watering flowerbeds and stretches of grass. On Friday, as he rode an ATV and dragged a small grader down gravel and wood-chip paths, the entire Faire spat out billows of dust.

He growled past a long line of exhibitor stalls called Smithy Row—blacksmith, silversmith, gunsmith, knifesmith—then followed the broad curve that fronted the falconer's station and turned up Artisan Row. He'd rolled past the stalls of a stonecutter, belter, embroiderer, and several painters when he felt a small spring of delight. Ginger Erlinger, the weaver, was here, puttering around in an open-faced hut flanked by a potter and basket maker. Ginger was a thirty-something single mom who'd become like a big sister to Jess and was certainly the best friend he'd made at the Faire. She even sent Joel care packages, although the two had never met.

Aside from Mig and Red, and a handful of casual tricks, Ginger Erlinger was the only person on earth who knew Jess was gay.

She was just as delighted to see him as he was to see her.

"Hey, Jesse," she called out, waving to him as he came to a stop. Her hair, a riot of tangerine-colored frizz, was pulled up and cinched at the top of her scalp. It looked like her head had erupted into a psychedelic mushroom cloud.

Grinning, Jess entered her stall and got the hug he'd anticipated. Aside from Ginger's primary loom, which took center stage, the space also contained a tabletop inkle loom, an array of strange-looking wooden tools, and various rustic racks and shelves for displaying her finished products. There was a spinner two stalls down, and Ginger sometimes bought yarn from her.

"You have time to visit for a while?" she asked, even as she bustled around preparing for the weekend.

"Do *you*?"

Ginger flapped a hand. "Oh hell yeah. There isn't much I have to do. Want some lemonade? You look parched." Without waiting for an answer, she lifted a thermal jug from the plank floor and grabbed two plastic cups from a large woven shoulder bag that hung from a chair.

They sat at one of the less cluttered tables and did some

catching up. Jess wondered for the umpteenth time if he should try hooking Ginger up with his dad, but the old man would've probably bored the snot out of her.

Once again Mig invaded his mind, and Jess realized how powerfully opposites could attract.

"I need your advice," he said before he had a chance to censor himself.

Ginger lifted her eyebrows. "Now why do I get the feeling it has to do with your love life?"

A corner of Jess's mouth lifted. "Shit, I really feel juvenile."

"Don't," Ginger said. "Whether you're eighteen or eighty, Jessbird, romance can be a mind-boggling bitch."

She called him Jessbird because she'd once had an older lover named Jasper whom Jess supposedly resembled. He didn't care *what* Ginger called him. He liked her and valued her friendship.

"Yeah, I guess." Jess leaned forward, resting his arms on his thighs. "Okay. Say you really like somebody, really admire him and enjoy his company, but there's someone else you don't like so much who keeps coming on to you."

Ginger lowered the cup from her mouth. "Sexually?"

"Uh… yeah." Jess hoped like hell he wasn't blushing. He took off his straw hat and fanned his face, as if he were flushed from the heat. "Until the come-ons are making you crazy and you can't keep resisting. You feel like a trout in one of those pay-to-fish ponds, bait constantly being dangled in front of you, and pretty soon you can't help snapping at it. But after you do—"

"You hate yourself."

Jess nodded. He pushed back the wave of hair that swept from his side-part and threatened to fall in a sweaty hank over his eyes.

"You're still on the fresh side of twenty, right?"

"Yeah."

"Well, *pfff*, that explains it. Guys your age are six-hundred-fifty BHP of horny. That doesn't make you an asshole without a conscience."

Jess's clipped laugh was sardonic. Asses and assholes—and how dicks responded to them—were what this whole mess was about. And, contrary to what Ginger said, not even the ghost of a conscience was involved.

"Why are you scoffing?" she asked, brushing grains of windblown dust off of her printed cotton skirt.

"Because I don't want to go through life being controlled by my hormones. Jesus. That would *really* be messed up. I might've already ruined something good."

"Can't you get your relief through the person you like? That's the most logical solution."

"I know," Jess said. "But we just don't have any privacy. We both live with our parents." Where could he and Mig go? They were both too busy, and their lives too subject to their families' scrutiny, to make regular trips to motels in other towns.

"Aw, you look so troubled." Ginger reached toward Jess and tucked back another strand of wayward hair. "Every problem has a solution, hon. You just need to decide what you want more: casual sex or commitment. You need to figure out which brings you more joy and satisfaction. Honestly, Jessbird, you have to take a good long look at yourself and where you're at in life. If you do that, answers will come."

Feeling hopeless, Jess heaved a sigh. Hell, he didn't have any experience with romance. He barely had any experience with sex. How could he even begin to judge what he wanted and needed most? And how could he know what standards to go by?

"I'm not even sure I can do *that*," he said. "I just... I don't seem to have any perspective."

"Hey, the scales will always tip in favor of what enriches your life. That's the thing you'll end up choosing. Because that's what'll make you feel good about yourself."

"Thanks for listening," Jess said. "Again."

Ginger gave him a reassuring smile. "You know it isn't a problem, baby."

Jess finished his lemonade and got up. "I better get back to work before Klingman sees me."

Ginger rose, too, and they hugged again. "Keep me posted," she said, then shook his arm. "Don't worry yourself into the ground. Nobody ever sees the light when they let *that* happen."

Jess's fog of confusion had thinned a little. From last weekend until now, it had swaddled his brain like one of Aunt Celeste's hand-knit scarves. *"Nobody ever sees the light when they let that happen."*

Wasn't that the damned truth?

Okay, fuck it. Given his dismal shortage of reference points, he'd just have to proceed on instinct. At the very least, he had to shitcan all the moping and go back to living. That was the starting point; that was the only way to discover what "enriched" his life.

CHAPTER 9

EVERY Friday night kicked off with the same ritual: The three Bonner boys piled into the old man's PT Cruiser and drove just over two miles to the Mariners Inn for a fish fry. Almost invariably, they were home by seven—early enough for the old man to kick back with his remote and his newspaper, and for Jess to go out, and for Red to work at wearing off his fingerprints on the keypad of his phone—something that would certainly benefit him once he embarked on his life of crime.

This week's outing began inauspiciously enough. As Jess mentally tossed around his options for the evening, Red chattered about going to the county fair with his inner circle of nitwit buddies and making sure Umfy ate enough "corn doggage" and funnel cakes to hurl on one of the rides. But then, as the Bonners got settled in around their table, the usual chitchat about Dad's job or Jess's job, Mom's last call or Joel's last letter was supplanted by the subject of dating.

Fucking dating.

It all started when a new waitress tried flirting with Jess... and Red tried not to choke on the ketchup-coated French fries that sacked out his cheeks.

For the last few years, Jess had managed to skate around the subject whenever it arose. He had convenient excuses for the lack of romance in his life: school, work, his youth (which, he claimed, made him more amenable to group socializing than to courtship).

Plus (he also claimed), he'd never had a relationship that was serious enough to justify introducing a girl to his family.

"She's cute," the old man noted with a smirk. "And she's really trying to get your attention. You should ask her out, Jesse. Looks like you've already got half the battle won."

Jess glanced at Red, expecting to see him expel a fry or two through his nose. "Uh… I'm not good at doing that sort of thing in front of people."

"Especially guys," Red mumbled as his mouth churned. He gave it more fodder by shoveling in some coleslaw.

Jess ignored him. "Besides, she looks a little old for me."

"Not by much," Dad said. "Twenty, twenty-two at the most." He actually winked. *Winked.* "Maybe you could benefit from her experience."

Red coughed. A few bits of coleslaw flew from his lips like confetti and landed on his slice of rye bread. He grabbed his water glass and drank.

"Are you all right?" the old man asked with genuine concern.

The kid nodded.

Jess rolled his eyes. Time to grab the metaphorical steering wheel and force this vehicle in another direction. "Speaking of dating, how are things going with that woman you met at the Dembrowskis' last week?"

"That was slick," Red forced out.

The old man tapped his chin, indicating Red should get acquainted with his napkin.

Jess had the impression dear Dad was stalling. "Well?"

"She's younger than me, not older. And her name is Natalia."

"Have you asked her on a date? That's a pretty name, by the way." So far, so good. The old man's attention was now on his own

79

discomfiture, not on Jess's love life. His cheeks had even gone rosy.

"Actually, I'm taking her out tomorrow evening. The races."

Jim's sons exchanged surprised glances. Jess braced himself. No way would Red be able to keep his mouth shut about *this* development.

Wait for it… Wait for it….

"Too bad you can't double date with Mom and whoever she's doin' now. Wouldn't that be—?"

Dad gave him The Look. With rapiers attached. This time, he didn't have to speak Jared's name to get his point across.

"DUDE, you can't keep dodging that bare lightbulb forever," Red told Jess after they'd returned home. "The interrogators won't give up, you know. You're in for the big-time third degree if you don't cough up a chick pretty soon."

"I don't recall asking for your advice." Jess strode around his room, searching for his car keys. He finally found them under the open copy of the Adams book.

"I'm trying to help you!" Red protested. "Where are you going?"

"Out."

"Can I come along?"

"No."

"Why? You gonna be doin' fag stuff?"

Hearing the word was like pulling the pin on a grenade Jess didn't realize he had secreted inside himself. He spun toward Red and slapped him. Hard. Harder than he'd ever thought he could hit anybody. Stunned by his own ferocity, he watched in horror as a field of scarlet flared across Red's skin, as his face pinched together and tears welled in his eyes.

"Oh shit," Jess whispered, gathering his little brother into his arms, holding him close.

"I'm sorry, Jesse." Red sounded as if the last five years had been stripped off his life. He was genuinely a kid again, achingly fragile, and Jess held him even tighter, as if Red would disintegrate if Jess let him go.

"I'm re-really sorry." Penitent beyond any capacity for penitence he'd ever shown before, Red kept crying into Jess's shoulder. His hands felt like catcher's mitts hanging from a clothesline as they gripped and weighted down the back of Jess's shirt.

"*Shhh.* I know." Soothingly, Jess petted Red's hair. "I'm sorry too. God, am I ever. I was totally out of line."

Red snurffled—a big, juicy inhalation of snot and breath. After a minute he pulled back and wiped at his eyes but kept them lowered. "I wasn't thinking," he mumbled to his shoes. "The guys say stuff like that all the time." He glanced up. "You know? But I didn't mean nothin' by it, and they don't mean nothin' by it either."

Nodding, Jess drew a hand down the side of Red's face.

"It still sucks, though. I gotta retrain my mouth."

Sadly, Jess smiled. "Are you okay?"

"Yeah."

"I didn't mean to hurt you. Honest, I didn't. It won't ever happen again."

More tears spilled silently down Red's cheeks.

"Oh fuck." Jess grabbed a clean T-shirt off his dresser and gently wiped the kid's face. The only other times he'd seen his brother so morose were when his mutt Clifford had died and, before that, when Mom had split.

Red grabbed a section of the T-shirt and blew his nose. "I'm

81

sorry I'm straight."

Jess coughed out a laugh. "What are you talking about?"

"Just what I said. I mean it."

"Hey, you can't help how you are. You were born that way."

Finally, they both let tentative smiles break through.

THERE was only one convenience store in Cold Harbor, and on a weekend night it was busier than a brothel. Running into somebody there and getting an impromptu invite to go partying was far less of a hassle, and an embarrassment, than calling one acquaintance after another out of sheer desperation. So Jess struck out for the Harbor Mart.

He was too restless to stay at home, especially after having lost his temper with Red. He needed some entertaining diversion. At least, that was what Jess told himself. But he knew damned well why he was driving into town.

He was hoping to run into Mig. Seeing him at the Harbor Mart was a long shot, but it was a shot.

Plenty of people were out and about. They were mostly weekenders picking up beer and bait, maps and lottery tickets, overpriced bread and milk. A smattering of surly straight boys, younger than Jess, milled around in the parking lot. When couples pulled up, either the guy or girl would dash into the store, grab something, and dash out again. The whole scene was kind of depressing, populated as it was by strangers, and Jess realized he shouldn't have wasted the gas.

He bought five dollars' worth of scratch-offs and Powerball tickets and resigned himself to another night at home. Sometimes it took a little jaunt like this to remind himself that being alone wasn't the worst thing in the world. Getting stupid with a bunch of guys he'd barely known in high school or tagging along with smoochy couples were far greater torments. And more painful testaments to his outsider status.

When someone yanked at the back of Jess's shirt as he was exiting the store, his blood surged with anticipation. He turned around as soon as he'd passed through the door. But it wasn't Mig whose face he saw amid the flow of people and lights and moths. Of course it wasn't. Mig was more of a toucher than a grabber.

"Where've you been?" asked Tomby.

Jess's spirit seemed to seep through the cracks in the sidewalk. "Working."

Tomby sipped at something in a large covered cup as her eyes ceaselessly scanned the shoppers and loiterers. "I mean weekends and evenings."

"Staying home."

One of the wannabe gangstas called over to Tomby. "Hey, bounce on over here, baby!"

Jess looked down and snorted. *Baby*... coming from a kid with barely perceptible fuzz beneath his nose and a voice still brittle from its change.

"Can't you see I'm talking to somebody?" Tomby shot back.

"So? Whatcha doin' when you're finished talking?"

"None of your business."

"Why dontcha come talk to *us*?"

Jess stepped toward his car, hoping to use this opportunity to escape, but Tomby grabbed his arm.

"Just wait, okay?" she hissed.

As the bad boys grinned and exchanged muttered words that likely weren't very flattering to Tomby, Jess felt both pity and concern for her—at least, enough to make him pause, and enough to make him tractable. He let Tomby lead him to a picnic table stationed at one end of the building.

"You really shouldn't be cruising around by yourself at night," he said, leaning his butt against the table edge. He didn't want to get too comfortable. But he didn't want to leave Tomby alone, either. "I'll give you a ride home if you need one."

"Save it, Jesse. I'm not a kid." After loudly vacuuming the bottom of her cup with her straw, she tossed them into a nearby trash can. "Besides, I'm waiting for someone."

Jess stood up. "In that case—"

Again, Tomby locked a hand onto his forearm. "Dude, will you just hold on a minute? I wanted to ask you something."

"What?"

"How come Mig didn't invite me to his birthday party? And why does Bran feel dissed by you? And, for that matter, when are we all getting together again?"

After raking a hand through his hair and sighing, Jess lowered his ass to the picnic table's bench. This was as good a time as any to clue her in about a few things. "Okay, listen. I'm having a really busy summer and I'll be having a really busy fall. Then the holidays are going to be here. Then I'm going to school. There's no place in my schedule for the Domino Club or the Ding Dong Club or any goddamn club. And I'm not *interested* in any goddamn club." Jess paused to gauge Tomby's reaction. Staring down at him, she looked both puzzled and displeased, as if he'd spoken with a foreign accent.

"And?"

"We're not on Sunrise Street anymore, Tomby. We don't need to climb into a tree house to talk about or do naughty things. I'm ready to move on. I shouldn't speak for Dylan, but I think he is too."

"Dylan?" she echoed in an arch tone.

Shit, Jess hadn't even been aware he'd used Mig's real name.

Maybe, subconsciously, it was another way of distancing the two of them from this childish bullshit.

Or maybe it was something else.

"Seems you and Mig are getting pretty tight." Tomby was haughty now; she must have interpreted Jess's words as a put-down, although he hadn't intended that. "Aren't you?"

Jess got up. "We're good friends. I hope we're always good friends."

As he walked away, he wondered if his voice had given away all he felt.

CHAPTER 10

EVERYTHING was different now. And the changes just kept coming.

Jess wondered what he'd been dreaming as he opened his eyes to another weekend, to a Saturday that tried shoving its optimistic sunshine through the navy-blue curtains on his bedroom window. He'd never before awakened with some realization stuck in his head, except for a superficial one like *I better get started on that civics essay* or *damn, I'm horny*.

Today, though, every thought that skirled through his mind seemed to have some import, and Jess felt strangely unsettled before he even swung his legs off the bed.

By the time he made his way to the kitchen, which was always the next stop after the bathroom, he felt somewhat calmed. The smell of coffee greeted him, and a song from the radio, and the strange sound of the old man alternately whistling and singing along to "I Feel for You."

"I didn't know you liked Chaka Khan," Jess said as he went to the refrigerator. He couldn't help smiling. Every time the corners were buffed off his father's squareness, he had to smile.

Startled, the old man turned away from the counter, where he'd nearly spilled the coffee he was pouring. "I've always liked Chaka Khan." He grinned. "If you were as cool as I am, you'd like Chaka Khan too."

What the fuck?

Red, who was just finishing his breakfast, rolled his eyes and shook his head. "You shoulda seen him playing air guitar."

"To Van Halen," Dad said.

Jess pulled a package of toaster waffles out of the freezer. "Let me guess. 'Jump'." He got a plate out of the cupboard, then reached for the last few strips of bacon, cooling now on a platter beside the stove.

"He's going to the races, all right," Red said, carrying his plate and silverware to the dishwasher.

Oh yeah, that explained it. Jumpin' Jim Bonner had a date tonight. Maybe he was hoping to get lucky.

Jess felt closer to normal now. The kid was his usual cocky self, the old man was unusually bubbly, and the sun looked a lot better pouring through the patio doors than stealing through a gap in his curtains.

"Red," the old man said as the kid reached for his cap, "pay attention while you're running the mower today. I don't want to see any more junk caught in the blades. And be sure to hose it off when you get back."

"Whose lawns are you chopping up?" Jess asked his brother, who was getting his cap situated just right on his head: bill backward and skewed off to one side.

"Kallmachers' and Chesters'. Oh, crap." Red hurried over to one of the lower cabinets and slid out a box of dog biscuits that he'd bought with his own hard-earned money. "Can't forget to bring treats for Dopey."

Jess smiled as he watched Red hustle out the door. *We should get him another dog*, he thought, then felt an upsurge of fresh guilt over what had happened last night.

"Would you mind running up to Ginke's after breakfast?" Dad asked as Jess waited for the toaster to eject his waffles.

"No, not at all. What do you need?"

GINKE'S was the only show in town when it came to hardware, sporting goods, and garden supplies. Shoppers who didn't feel like wasting time and gas getting to one of the big chain stores flooded Ginke's aisles from Monday morning through Saturday afternoon.

After scanning the old man's list, Jess grabbed a handheld basket and went straight to the electrical section. He knew the store's layout like the landscape of his dick. Within minutes he had what he needed.

After dawdling for a while in the crafts corner, trying to find a little something for Red, he grabbed a box of multicolored, glow-in-the-dark chalk and headed for the checkout. But he didn't make it there.

Out of the corner of his eye, Jess glimpsed a familiar form in an aisle full of plumbing fixtures. Squaring his shoulders, he turned right. He forced himself to saunter rather than sprint.

"Hey, how're things going?" he said cheerily, aware of his shortness of breath.

"Oh, hi." Mig shrugged. "Pretty good. Same old stuff."

Was he being standoffish? Jess couldn't tell.

Because, oh shit, how weak he felt at the sight of Mig, at merely the sight of his eyelids raising and lowering, which drew Jess's attention to those thick black lashes. He adored Mig's eyelashes. He wanted to swipe the tip of his tongue along each delicate row.

The urge wasn't sexual. Jess didn't know what it was, aside from mildly perverse. Flustered, he searched for something to say.

Mig beat him to it. "What, uh… what're you getting?" He motioned toward the small basket Jess clutched in his left hand.

Jess lifted it. "Electrical parts. I'm helping the old man with some work around the house today." He smiled, but his mouth felt jumpy. "Father-son bonding and all that crap. Red's out with the mower, terrorizing neighbors' lawns. He might pitch in when he gets back. If he doesn't dick around getting twine or some other junk off the mower blades. Which he almost always does."

Jesus, zip it, why dontcha!

If Mig noticed how nervous Jess was, he didn't let on. Instead, he laughed quietly at the reference to Red, who'd been an endless source of amusement to both of them since those golden days on Sunrise Street. "Yeah, I've got projects too. I don't think my father's going to be helping, though."

Jess shifted his stance. Before, he couldn't seem to stop his mouth from running. Now, he couldn't seem to start it up again.

"Mig… Dylan…."

Mig's gaze jumped to Jess's face.

Jess lowered his voice to a murmur. "Are you busy this evening?"

Immediately Mig lowered his gaze, those gorgeous lashes making him look both demure and alluring. "Bran invited me over."

"What?"

Sheepishly, Mig smiled. "Sorry. Just gigging you a little."

Relief washed through Jess. "I guess I deserve it." He risked cupping Mig's forearm, but only briefly. Mig's skin was still warm from the summer sun. "Want to get together tonight? Maybe we could catch a movie or something."

Mig's gaze shifted to the store shelves, cluttered with metallic and plastic shapes heaped in bins or hung from hooks. "Let's go talk in the parking lot, okay?"

After they checked out and Jess threw the bag of outlets and switches into his car, which was parked on the street in front of Ginke's, he threaded down the narrow walkway between the hardware store and Pots 'n' Petals, the florist's shop next-door. Mig's pickup was in Ginke's rear lot, sitting near a flight of wooden stairs that led to a second-story apartment. Jess wondered vaguely if it might be for rent—and if he should mention that possibility to Mig.

They sat on the gate of Mig's truck. Across the alley that ran behind the Main Street stores, small residential backyards erupted with grills, flowerbeds, and blindingly colorful play sets.

Mig resituated his ballcap, a piece of apparel now near and dear to Jess's heart. Again he wanted to touch the rebellious dark curls that crept out beneath its edges. Fuck, what was *with* him? It couldn't have just been horniness. His sexual appetite had never before come bundled with sentimentality over articles of clothing.

"Was there something specific you wanted to talk about?" Jess asked hopefully.

Mig took a big breath before looking at him. "Yeah, I guess. I really don't wanna get in the habit of sweeping stuff under the carpet. God knows I do enough of that with my parents."

"I know. So do I."

"So it's important to get things out in the open."

"I agree." This wasn't sounding so good. Anxiety scurried through Jess's stomach as he waited for Mig to explain.

Somewhere in the nearby neighborhood, a child squealed in delight. Jess heard a splash. A babel of young, happy voices followed. *The sounds of innocence*, Jess thought... just as Mig began to speak.

"This is hard for me, Jesse." Mig stared at the backyards beyond Ginke's parking lot, stress gathering in his face.

"What is? Talking to me?"

"No. I like talking with you."

"Then what's hard for you?"

Mig slid him a glance. "Figuring out things that are bothering me. Then explaining myself. Then... following through."

"Whatever it is, it sounds important."

"To me it is." With a muted groan, Mig rocked backward, knees raised, and palmed the bill of his cap over his eyes. "Shit. You're gonna think I'm a little girl."

"What?" Jess laughed. He tugged Mig upright by pulling on the leg of his jeans. "Believe me, I'll *never* think of you as a little girl." He looked into Mig's eyes, and his tone lowered. "Never."

A conduit opened. Only for a couple of seconds, though. Only long enough for them both to realize it was there and for Mig to resist it. At least that was what Jess sensed.

"Maybe it wouldn't be good for us to hang out together," Mig said. "For a while, anyway."

Jess's face fell. "Why?"

His immediate assumption had to do with the fact they were gay, that Mig was bothered by the risks they'd taken and was worried they might take more. Certain words, looks, touches— *anything* could make people suspicious.

After taking a minute to gather his thoughts, Mig said, "Because I… because maybe we want different things."

Well, Jess had called *that* one wrong. He tried to reorient his thinking to catch Mig's drift, but it kept eluding him. "That's natural," he said with an uncertain smile. "Even best friends for life don't want exactly the same things. People are individuals."

"No, I mean…." Mig had begun to look genuinely pained, and Jess was even more in the dark, even more nettled by anxiety. "I don't want us to get too close. You know? You're already really smart, and you'll be going off to school in January to get even smarter—"

"Educated," Jess corrected. "There's a difference."

"Whatever. But I'll be staying here and not getting educated about much of anything. And before you go you'll be doing your man-whore thing." He shot Jess a glance. "Which I understand, 'cause I been there myself, but I've kinda started to realize that maybe I want more than that, maybe certain things are important to me that ain't important to other guys our age, and it'd better for me if I kinda pulled back and—"

Jess gripped Mig's knee. "Hey, slow down."

"Man, I knew I'd fuck this up," Mig muttered.

"You're not fucking anything up." *You're afraid of something. That's what it is. Afraid of being left behind, of not being good enough, some stupid goddamned thing like that.* But Jess couldn't voice his interpretation. That would've embarrassed the hell out of Mig, and he seemed embarrassed enough as it was. "Mig, I'd hate it if we stopped being friends."

"That's not what I'm talking about," he said with obvious frustration. "I think we should just… not spend too much time together, do our own thing for a while. It'll help us figure out what we're about. You know? And if we really *are* friends, we'll get together again. 'Cause that's how it works."

Jess blinked. The reflex startled him when he realized why it was happening: because tears stung the backs of his eyes. He'd just begun to discover Dylan Finch, the grown-up Dylan Finch, and he very much liked what he'd seen and most definitely wanted to see more. Only… the feeling didn't seem to be mutual.

What had gone wrong?

"Have I done something to piss you off? Was it that… scene with Brandon?"

Mig shook his head, swallowed. "No."

Jess stared at his lowered face, at the profile he thought was not only incomparably handsome but nuanced with maturity. Suddenly, Mig seemed a lot older than the rest of the people in their graduating class. And a lot more full of feeling.

"I'm not saying I think you're an asshole or a bad influence or anything like that." When, abruptly, Mig looked at Jess again, the strain was evident in his face. "I just think we gotta figure out what

what's important to us. It's like how we see the Domino Club. There's no sense in hanging on to something from your past if it ain't right for you anymore."

As if Mig's words had given him a push, Jess jumped off the truck gate. "Okay." He was hurt. And resented being hurt. And wanted it to stop.

Mig reached for him. "Jess—" He forced a smile. "Hey, I'm not pissin' on you. Honest. Just think about what I said. Maybe it'll make sense once you think about it. All I'm saying is, we're kind of at this crossroads—"

"And you think you're going one way and I'm going another."

"Maybe."

Jess rubbed a hand over his suddenly-tired eyes. "Is it all right if we still talk on the phone once in a while?" Unintended sarcasm tinctured the question. He had to hide behind *something*.

"Sure it is. Shit, Jess, it ain't... it isn't like I think you're some stain I got to bleach from my life."

"Thanks. That's good to know." The sarcasm was more than a tincture now.

Mig's brows were drawn. Troubled and exasperated, he flung up his arms. "I don't how to say what I mean, okay? You wanna hate me for that, go ahead and hate me!"

Damn it, Jess thought, *why am I being such a dick?* He allowed himself a wan smile as he clapped the side of Mig's knee. "That'll never happen."

They lingered in silence for an awkward moment. Jess slid a hand into his pocket and grabbed his key ring. "All right, I'll think about what you said."

He didn't particularly want to think about it. In fact, Jess suspected he'd try his damnedest not to. Being told to get lost didn't allow for too many positive interpretations.

Damn it, why couldn't they get their shit straight?

93

SINCE Jess had to put in six hours at the Ren Faire on Sunday, he didn't even entertain the thought of going out on Saturday night. Instead, he shot hoops with Red and his buddies in the driveway until nightfall. Jess wasn't much of a basketball player, but the doofuses Red hung out with at least kept his mind off other things.

Umfy Randall was there, of course, and he proved as spry as Bigfoot after Thanksgiving dinner. Umfy had got his nickname by challenging people to punch him in his ironclad, dome-shaped gut. Although he barely flinched when he took a hit, he invariably let out an *oomph*.

Jess declined Umfy's invitation to sock him. His guilt over slapping Red was still too fresh.

Two-tone Fontaine had come over as well. He was a lanky, good-looking boy whose mother was Native American—Oneida or, as Two-tone said without a stutter, Haudenosaunee—and whose father was white. "Don't you find the name *Two-tone* a little offensive?" Jess asked him. And Two-tone laconically replied, "Beats the oolang out of 'half-breed'." After which Red added, "Makes him sound like a race car. Don't you think he kind of looks like one?" Puzzled, Jess said no, and didn't bother asking what "oolang" was, even though that word was stranger than Red's comparison.

Flushed with exertion, Umfy stuck his hand toward Two-tone. "Lone Ranger says, 'Pull my finger, Kemo Sabe.'"

"I'd only do it if I knew silver dollars were gonna pour out of his butt," Red muttered. He spun toward the basket like an unraveling tornado and tried to execute a dunk. All he managed to do was slam his wrist against the steel hoop and send the ball flying in the opposite direction.

Two-tone grabbed the ball out of the air. "I wouldn't do it at all." Gracefully, he leapt into a quarter-turn and bounced the ball, hard, off Umfy's belly. "Tonto says, 'Fuck off, fat white boy full of stink.'"

As soon as the ball hit Umfy, something came out of his ass… but it sure didn't jingle like silver dollars.

Chuckling, Jess shook his head.

The phrase *politically correct* was not a part of these kids' vocabularies. But neither, thank God, was the word *prejudice*. Jess thought Cold Harbor's non-Caucasian residents were probably more accepted than gay folks would ever be. He knew he could've been wrong, but he wasn't ready to find out. Not just yet.

After he told the boys his intended major in college, they spun off on a tangent about the brain of Charlie Sheen—a discussion that added nothing to Jess's stock of knowledge and, in fact, may have detracted from it. That was when he knew he'd be better off in bed.

At least he was tired. At least he wouldn't have to lie there, suffering brain strain as he tried to come to terms with Mig's rejection.

MIG

"DYLAN, aren't you going out tonight?"

Mig's mother, who'd been walking past his room, stood in the doorway and regarded him as he sat cross-legged on the bed. Although her look was mostly quizzical, it held a touch of displeasure.

He glanced away from the TV that sat on his dresser. "No. I decided not to."

"You've been staying in your room a lot lately."

"Maybe I have." Mig shrugged. "I never thought about it." Great. Just what he needed—being under a microscope. It was one of the many things that sucked about being an only child. He really had to get his own place.

"There's still no girl who's caught your eye?" His mother attempted a smile. "You have to spend all that money you're making on *someone*."

"Yeah, myself." Cool. She'd just given him a reason for not dating. "I'm saving everything I can for my apartment. Security deposit, first and last months' rent, furniture, all kinds of stuff. That's not small change, Mom. And buying the truck already set me back."

Her expression softened toward sympathy. "Your dad and I are willing to help, you know."

"I know. But I don't want your help."

Sighing, she rested a hand on the doorknob. "I just hate to see you becoming a hermit. Boys your age *should* go out and have fun."

Believe me, Mom, you don't want me having the kind of fun I want to have. The thought gave Mig a sick feeling.

"Maybe you should think about joining the youth group at church. They always have something going on. And Lord knows you'll meet better-quality people than you will through Brandon Nygaard." Her tone had taken on an edge Mig knew well, although she always tried to blunt it.

Mig stretched out his legs, adjusted his back against the pillows, and lifted the remote. "You have to stop worrying about me. I know what I'm doing."

His mother slipped him a final half-smile and quietly closed the door.

Bullshit, he thought. *I don't have a* clue *what I'm doing.*

Yeah, he had the job thing down. And the saving-money thing. But his social life? That was a bigger clusterfuck than a tangled trawling net.

Mig closed his eyes for a minute and immediately saw Jess.

"God, you're an idiot," he whispered to himself.

He'd been determined to speak plainly to Jess, to tell it like it was. That was the only way to make your position clear, regardless of how you might cringe at being open—so open you could feel wind-borne sand scouring your insides. But when he'd had his chance in Ginke's parking lot, he couldn't speak the whole truth. He didn't know how. He'd danced around the issue, trying to get his point across without sounding like some calf-eyed fourteen-year-old girl. He hadn't wanted to make Jess so uncomfortable he'd drop an ax through whatever connection they had.

He'd wanted to save himself but hadn't known how to express his need for salvation.

I have feelings for you, and I don't think it's good for me to have feelings for you. It ripped me up to see you with Bran. So maybe if we stop spending time together, the feelings will go away. What the fuck kind of man ever said shit like that?

Damn. How much more gay could he get?

At least that was what any eavesdropper would've thought. And maybe what Jess would've thought. *Jesus, Mig, can't we just do each other and enjoy it? Can't we just tap one kind of sap without tapping the other?*

Well, Jess wouldn't have had that exact thought—he wasn't coldhearted—but the confession would've left him discombobulated and wary. Especially the part about Brandon. Guys their age were supposed to play around. Mig just wasn't like most guys their age. Even when he seemed to be, he wasn't.

He rested his head against the pillows and again closed his eyes. Maybe he should try. Maybe he should slide on back to Tricksville, where he'd been before Jess Bonner had made him think all his fondest fantasies could come true.

Having a sex life wasn't like having a love life, but it sure beat wasting away in his parents' house.

CHAPTER 11

ALTHOUGH the heat wasn't nearly as scorching as it had been throughout the week—or, worse yet, as it had been in July—there was more than enough summer in the sultry air to leave Jess wrung out and sweating by the end of his shift.

Before changing into his street clothes and heading out, he sat on a tall wood stool just outside the stable doors and lazily watched the sparse flow of human and animal traffic at this far end of the grounds. A college-age girl whose name Jess couldn't remember shuffled toward one of the adjacent pens, her arms spread wide and a stick in each hand. She was supposedly dressed like a shepherdess, although it was four unruly miniature goats she was trying to lead. Smart and sassy, those little buggers had more personality than a lot of people Jess knew.

Two of them stopped in their tracks and engaged in a head-butting match. Jess smiled. One time when Red had been there with Dad, he'd suggested the Faire should hire Umfy, outfit him with a helmet, and pit him against a full-size goat. *"A show every couple hours. It would be a real crowd pleaser,"* Red had asserted, and Dad had answered, *"Maybe it would knock some sense into him too."*

Jess tipped the Coke bottle to his lips and drank.

From beneath his lowered eyelids, he saw a passerby, a thirtyish man likely on his way to the restrooms, continually shooting glances his way.

Had the guy been lying on a beach, Jess thought, he would've been virtually invisible. He had sand-colored hair and sand-colored eyebrows, and even his skin, which probably spent the summer shielded by sunscreen, hadn't browned past the medium-beige stage. The powder blue shirt hanging casually over his tan safari shorts was his only concession to color.

Jess recognized the style of the shirt. His maternal grandfather had a closet full of those babies.

He noted the length of the shorts. Straight guys shunned so abbreviated an inseam.

"Guayabera?" Jess called out, dropping his gaze to the man's shirt and nodding at it.

The guy smiled with greasy ease and sauntered over, his hands in his pockets. "Yes, as a matter of fact." He watched the Coke bottle as Jess put it to his mouth. Or rather, watched Jess's mouth kiss the bottle's lip. "I'm surprised you recognize the brand. Most college kids aren't familiar with classic clothing."

Okay, game on. "I'm not in college." Jess rested the bottle at a casual angle between his hip and groin. His free hand rested directly opposite. The cut of his work chaps did the rest of the framing. "Not yet, anyway."

The man's smile shrank by a fraction of a degree. "Oh. You look about that age."

"I'm eighteen. I'll be starting second semester." Jess intuitively understood the need for such clarification. Only pedophiles and pederasts sought out underage boys. Chicken hawks liked 'em young but legal. This dude, judging by his dress and demeanor, fell in the latter category. If Jess had to put money on it, he'd bet the guy was a professional who lived in a suburb of Chicago.

Yeah, he was the type who'd collapse and cry in a corner if he was perceived as a child molester, even though he'd likely ogled his share of fourteen- to seventeen-year-old twinks. Jess had encountered several such men at the Faire. He'd ignored all but one.

They made small talk for a while as *this* man, whose name was Dave, felt him out. Eagerness shivered beneath Dave's caution like a twitching muscle. He was a blandly good-looking guy, and Jess got a teensy bit more excited each time Dave's light-brown eyes dropped to Jess's open shirt or, more frequently, to the apex of his thighs.

"So, uh...." Dave drained the bottle of water he'd been carrying. "You on break?"

"Actually, my shift's over. I was just about to leave." Jess slid off the stool and took his time doing it.

Dave cleared his throat. "Your girlfriend's probably waiting for you, huh?" His next declaration teetered on a chortle that was strung taut as a tightrope. "Women don't like their men working on weekends."

"I wouldn't know," Jess said smoothly. They were almost there. Commitment lay in his next sentence, which he spoke in a lowered voice. "I've never had a girlfriend."

"Oh? Why's that?" Dave's desire undulated through the air and against Jess's body. "You don't like guys, do you?"

Jess smiled.

"Christ." Dave darted a look to the left, to the right, then over his shoulder for good measure. "Would you, uh...." He licked his lips. "Would you like to go somewhere, if there's a place to go?"

"Depends on what you have in mind." Amazing, Jess thought, how quickly mature, accomplished men ceded control to inexperienced cubs like himself when their brains slipped to their scrotums. Although he had no right to his sense of power, it still turned him on.

Dave leaned toward him, close enough for Jess to feel the heat of his breath and smell the residue of wine it bore. "I want to grip your ass while I suck your dick. I want to crawl between those long, lean legs and lick your tender balls. I want to feel you shoot in my mouth. That's what I have in mind."

Jess's breath came out harder. "Sounds like a plan. Follow me."

He didn't want to think about it; he just wanted to let it happen. His cock had already begun to swell against the thin, tight pants he wore beneath his chaps, and he hoped that if anybody noticed, they'd simply assume many of the Ren Faire costumes either crowded or emphasized men's packages.

Dave stared at his ass as he walked. Jess didn't need eyes in the back of his head to know that. He didn't even need to hear Dave's poorly suppressed, growly moans to know that. He had a nice ass, and that was knowledge enough.

There was a utility room sandwiched between the men's and women's restrooms in the same building Dave might've been heading toward. Although it was on the other side of the animal pens, which put it off the Faire's most heavily traveled paths, its cinderblock construction had still been dolled up on the outside. From afar, the building looked like a half-timbered structure with a thatched roof. From closer than ten yards, it looked like what it was. In fact, Jess had recently helped patch the thin stucco nogging that covered the gray and none-too-Elizabethan blocks.

Since it was a Sunday, no workers would have reason to enter the utility room unless some mess or malfunction required immediate attention. Routine cleanup was left for the weekday crew. Fairly confident they wouldn't be disturbed, Jess led Dave to the rear of the restroom building and separated a key from the dozen or so hanging from a ring he kept in his vest pocket.

The room was stifling, as if the blackness that packed it were spun from wool. Sweat immediately dewed along Jess's hairline and upper lip, on the span between his shoulder blades and in the shallow gully dividing his chest. Two small windows high in the wall on either side of the door were open but allowed for no cross-ventilation. Jess groped for a fan on one of the shelves and turned it on.

"Is there a light?" Dave whispered. "Even a dim one?" He

obviously wanted to see his catch.

Jess reached up and felt for the ceiling fixture's chain. The undersea glow cast by a single compact fluorescent bulb filled the room.

The space wasn't *too* cluttered—Jess and an older coworker named Maddie tried to keep it neat and organized—but there were still mops in scrub buckets and a variety of brooms and stepladders littering the floor. He didn't apologize for the ugliness of the accommodations. Anybody who wanted to suck cock as much as Dave did required no apologies.

Jess pulled the leather vest from his shoulders and tossed it aside. He got the chaps off his legs. His street clothes were in here anyway, since utility rooms and bathroom stalls were the places where he could change, so he might as well begin stripping down now.

"Your mouth really gets to me," Dave said in a husky murmur. He snapped open his shorts. "I don't usually want to kiss guys, but I'd love to make an exception right now."

"No. I don't know you. Just do what you said you wanted to do." Jess shoved down his pants, a graphic reminder.

"Oh Christ, that's fucking gorgeous." Mouth hanging open, Dave palmed the thick arch of Jess's cock within the pouch of his jock strap. His other hand slid to Jess's ass and fondled it, squeezed it, fondled it more urgently. The odor of sweat, dusty and pungent, rose more strongly from his body.

Beyond the wall opposite the door, a toilet flushed.

"There's a stepstool behind you and to the left," Jess said. "Set it up in front of me."

Dave's tongue had sort of curled under and inched toward his lips, as if it were swelling in his mouth. His harsh breathing managed to slide around it. "May I suck your nipples?" He pulled half of Jess's shirt to one side. "They're beautiful."

Jess flinched away. "No. Don't." He sometimes played with

his nipples when he was beating off, but he didn't think he'd like a stranger doing it. "Stay between my waist and knees."

Dave grabbed the stepstool and hurriedly pulled it open, then shoved his crisp but slightly-too-short shorts and soft but slightly-too-large briefs down his hips. An erection with more girth than length sprang up, a truly chubby chubby.

Unsteadily, Dave sat on the top of the stool, roughly pulled Jess forward by giving his ass a one-handed clutch, and took in what he was after. Simultaneously, he worked his own prick with vigor.

Jess shuddered. Every muscle between his belly and thighs seemed to contract as excitement sliced through him. He stared down as his hard-on disappeared, reappeared, disappeared between the hollows of Dave's cheeks.

It's good. It's good. It's good.

He wanted to grip Dave's head, make it nothing more than a big sleeve for his straining cock, but he couldn't bring himself to touch it, to feel the contours of Dave's skull or the texture of his hair. He couldn't.

So he lost himself to the tug and release, the feelgood insistence that reached down into his balls, up into his abdomen, and back into his spine. Dave resumed that weird, atonal humming, broken into dots and dashes by the physics of suction.

"I love it that guys your age are so easy," he murmured. "And so pretty. I love it. Oh sweet Jesus I love it." He slithered a hot, sweaty hand between Jess's legs and fingered his balls, slithered it farther back and traced the tight cleft of Jess's ass. "And you come so goddamned hard and so long."

Jess closed his eyes. He wanted to close his ears. His body was reacting to the stimulation—how could it not?—but this was nothing like his intimacy with Mig. Hell, this was nothing resembling intimacy. Jess could've been thrusting his erection into wet memory foam.

Dimly, he knew he'd feel sullied when this was over—he'd

felt that way the last times he'd caved in to such propositions —but Mig didn't want him and this closeted suburbanite did, and a penis in need didn't know the difference between a smutty suck and a sweetheart suck and... oh goddammit, why did his goddamn mind have to kick into gear while he was getting a goddamn blowjob?

Out of sheer desperation, he cinched his thumb and forefinger around the base of his shaft. A jagged release tore through him. He might've reflexively gripped Dave's head at that moment, maybe angrily gripped it, but at least he didn't register the feel of it. Dave sucked down everything Jess had to give—not only the splooge but the sudden flare of resentment, the disgust, the longing for someone else's face to be where Dave's face was, all shooting out, out and away....

"Delicious," Dave whispered as he got up.

Jess didn't look at him. He didn't know if Dave had come or not, or, if he had, where he'd wiped his hand. The only thing Jess cared about at the moment was getting the hell out of there.

"I'd like to give you something," Dave said as he put himself back together.

For the first time since they'd entered the room, Jess looked him full in the face. "I beg your pardon?"

Dave pulled a thin wallet out of his pocket. It was attached to one of his belt loops by a braided leather thong. He opened it, extracted a bill and what looked like a business card, and held up both between two fingers. The card was tucked within the folded currency. "I thought you might need a little something for your college fund."

"Sure. Okay." Numbly, Jess took the donation. "Thank you."

"You're welcome. You were quite an unexpected treat. I really, truly hope we can get together again sometime." After smiling in a way that chilled Jess, Dave cracked open the door, reconnoitered, then slipped outside.

Jess bagged up his shirt and work trousers to take home for a wash. He hung the vest and chaps on hooks at the rear of the room. Once he was dressed in his street clothes, he slipped the damp and now crumpled bill into his jeans pocket.

It was a C-note. One hundred dollars.

He'd just become a professional boy-toy.

His icy numbness gave way to a rolling wall of heat. Bolting outside, he vomited in the shrubbery behind the phony timber-framed building.

OUT of both habit and hope, Jess checked his phone for messages as soon as he got in his car. There was only one, from a sender called Make My Day E-Cards.

Fingers trembling, he opened it.

A tight cluster of glistening purple flowers appeared. Slowly, they opened into a bouquet. The masked figure of a man rose from the bouquet's center like a hatless Lone Ranger. He lifted one side of his mask and winked.

From a not-so-secret admirer read the line that appeared at the bottom of the viewing pane.

The week was off to a hell of a start.

CHAPTER 12

JESS flipped over onto his belly to let the sun roast his back. The lounge chair, open flat, squeaked and rocked beneath his weight.

What a pleasant change, having the house to himself and nothing pressing to do. Red was at the county fair with his friends. Dad was reclaiming his youth by rafting on some river with Natalia—who Red feared was "one of those skeezy Russian chicks that come up from Chicago to fish for an American husband." The kid said one of his classmates had acquired a stepmother that way, and she looked like a hooker.

A hooker....

Although it was nearly a week after his accidental foray into the world of prostitution, Jess didn't feel much better about himself. He'd put the hundred in the bank. He'd put Dave's business card and the details of their encounter in the trash. The card stayed there, but the memories kept jumping out and seizing him.

He needed to talk, get the incident off his chest, but he had no one to talk to. Not about that. Not about getting paid for shoving his dick down a stranger's throat while the stranger told him how young and pretty and easy he was.

Okay, the "young" part was true. The "pretty" part, although it struck Jess as condescending, was subjective. But the "easy"—that had stung, and it continued to rankle. Every time the word arose in Jess's mind, the greasy feel of that currency ghosted over his palm.

Worse yet, a different kind of feeling haunted him: the fear of becoming sexually self-serving and shallow. Like Brandon.

His fear seemed more than justified. Because, goddammit, being desired *was* a thrill, and being so strongly desired that it put you in control was a thrill on an ego trip, and getting paid for the thrill to be on that ego trip was....

Fucked up.

"Shit," Jess whispered.

He pulled his phone off the grass, lifted his sunglasses above his eyes, and checked for messages. Nothing.

Jess's "not-so-secret admirer" remained a mystery. He hadn't outed himself. Then again, the person might've been a girl. Jess's interaction with some of his female coworkers was borderline flirtatious, or could be construed that way. Another possibility was that Red was playing a joke on him.

In any case, Jess tried to toss that incident, too, into the trash. He didn't want to keep hoping Mig had sent the e-card; he didn't want to keep realizing it wasn't something Mig would do.

Inside the house, the landline phone rang. Jess lifted his head and squinted at the patio doors. When, after the third ring, the answering machine clicked on, he laid his head down again, face still turned toward the house. He let his right arm hang off the edge of the lounge, the cell phone loosely cupped in his hand.

It trilled just as he began to doze off. Startled, he jerked into alertness and clumsily tried to align the phone with his ear.

"Hullo."

"Jess, where's your father?"

Frowning, Jess boosted himself onto his elbows. "Mig?"

"Yeah. Is your dad home?"

"No, he's—"

"Are you working?"

"No, I'm just lying around." Jess turned over and sat up. Why the hell would Mig want to talk to his dad? And why did he sound so tense?

"Jess, you have to come to Manitowoc. The hospital. Shit, I can't think of its name."

Jess couldn't remember it either, except that it had a religious sound—Catholic, probably. He was already on his feet and sprinting into the house, his heart thundering. "What happened? Where are you?"

"I'm on my way to the emergency room. Just meet me there, okay?"

"Are you all right?" Jess stumbled and fell onto the bed as he tried to get his jeans on. His voice tightened and rose. "*Mig?*"

"I'm fine. You need to stay calm." A deep inhalation and exhalation came through the phone, as if Mig were trying to follow his own advice. "I was at the county fair—"

"The fair?" Jess repeated thinly. He froze midway through getting his shirt on. *Oh fuck. Oh no. No, please....*

"And I ran into Red with a few of his buddies."

Nearly paralyzed with panic, Jess had to force himself to focus and get moving again. Where the *fuck* were his shoes?

"They were all talking at once," Mig went on, "just sort of bending my ear about rides and crap, and all of a sudden Umfy Randall bolted off the path and into some bushes and started upchucking. Red and the other two guys were laughing, but they went after him. I was just walking away when Chad Fontaine came charging after me looking all upset, and he told me, 'Red got stung by some bees and he's—'"

"Having a reaction," Jess said with half a voice. His insides shriveled in terror at the words as he pulled a dusty pair of sandals out from under his bed. He hated sandals. "Did he stick himself with the EpiPen?"

"With what?"

"An injection thingy filled with epinephrine. He's supposed to carry one with him every time he goes outdoors in warm weather. If he gets stung, he has to jam it into his thigh." Jess found it increasingly difficult to keep his phone in place near his ear, listen, ask questions, process what Mig was telling him, and get his shit together.

"I don't think so," Mig said.

"Oh God...." *Don't panic. Keep it together, keep it together.*

"But when I got to him, Chad had already flicked the stingers out—I think there were three—and I gave him a couple of my antihistamine tablets and started carrying him to the first-aid station while I had one of the other guys call 9-1-1. But before we got there, a golf cart pulled up and took us the rest of the way. And yeah, they gave him a shot of something. Then the EMTs showed up and decided to take him to the hospital."

"Why are *you* going to the hospital? You don't have to." Jess had finally made it into the kitchen. He had his wallet and keys. *What else? What am I forgetting?*

"Yes I do," Mig said. "Red asked if I would come. He has no one else to be with him. His buddies are idiots, except maybe for that Fontaine kid. They'd probably just get in the way."

Jess paused as Mig's selflessness hit him. "Thank you," he said with quiet sincerity.

"It isn't a problem, Jesse. I don't mind at all. Just be careful driving."

"Okay. See you in a little while."

Jess's mind jumped from one thought to another as he finished doing what he had to do.

Why didn't that dopey kid take his EpiPen with him?

Chad, who's Chad? Oh...Fontaine. Two-tone. Did he know to get those stingers out because he's half Oneida? Do all Indians know shit like that?

At least Manitowoc's only a short hop along the lakeshore.

Mig...Mig carried him.

Jess ripped a piece of paper from the notepad next to the phone and scrawled *Come to M'woc hosp emergency room NOW*, then wondered how to make sure his father saw it. Just lying there on the center island, the paper was too small to draw immediate attention. So he grabbed a bowl of leftover spaghetti from the fridge, dumped it on the island's butcher-block surface, and propped the note upright at the top of the gooey orange heap. He fleetingly realized it was something Red would do. Just before he dashed out to the garage, he yanked the copy of his father's health insurance card off the refrigerator. The magnet that had held it in place clattered to the floor.

The calendar on the refrigerator door told him it was August 27th, a date he would never, for a number of reasons, forget.

JESS had never been in an emergency room. The quiet surprised him. This was nothing like the ERs, either real or made up, on television. No scurrying doctors and nurses with funny slippers over their shoes and stethoscopes flying off their chests as they raced about with weighty purpose. No barked orders or frantic shouts over screams of agony. No machines full of terrifying implications rolling down the hallway.

Just gleam. Everything around Jess seemed to shine. For a disorienting moment, he feared he was in the wrong place. No. He wasn't so spaced out he couldn't follow signs. Besides, the smell was right—that sickening, antiseptic tang.

He tried to take comfort in the fact that his dad would soon be there. The old man had called from home while Jess was on the road.

Queasiness crept into him as a headache thudded to life. Nerves and hunger and fluorescent lights—a ménage made in hell. He felt as if he'd taken a bad drug.

Where the hell was Red? Where was Mig?

Jess picked up his pace as he neared the reception desk. Breathless, he rested his forearms on the smooth, cool counter. He seemed to be peering down a tunnel; his eyes only took in whatever was right in front of him.

The fortyish woman behind the desk looked up, her pleasant expression neither too somber nor too perky. Her name tag read *Claire Chasen.*

"My brother's here. Jared Bonner. They brought him from the fair with anaphylaxis. How is he?"

"And your name is…?"

"Jesse Bonner."

"Did you know your brother Dylan was here, Jesse?"

Jess felt his eyebrows lift. "Uh… yes. He's the one who called me. Our father should be here soon. Oh, in the meantime…." He patted then dug into his pockets. "Here's his insurance card. I suppose it's more important to you people than anything else."

Weird, hearing Mig referred to as his brother. Creepy, actually, considering the incestuous overtones.

Ms. Chasen pursed her lips, most likely in umbrage, as she took the card. She was careful not to grab it too eagerly. "Why don't you have a seat," she said, pointing vaguely toward a waiting area. "One of our staff will come talk to you in a bit."

One of our staff. It was telling that Ms. Chasen hadn't used the word *doctor.* Was Red being treated by some nurse practitioner or

112

physician's assistant or one of those other care providers who was countless rungs down the ladder from a real MD?

And where in fucking hell was Mig?

"Can I see him?" Jess asked. "My little brother, I mean."

The question provoked a tight smile. "You'll have to wait. It shouldn't be long."

"Do you know where Dylan went?"

Ms. Chasen, who was entering information from Jim Bonner's insurance card, couldn't be bothered giving Jess a glance. "No, sorry."

Flustered, Jess looked down the hall and wondered if he should just try to find Red when nobody was watching. Office personnel and one guy in scrubs moved around the large room behind the reception desk, but aside from staff, nobody else was around.

The insurance card appeared on the counter. Ms. Chasen, who must've felt she'd done her duty, didn't speak. Jess wanted to throw up. He was angry and anxious and frustrated and in no mood to observe rules while he sat in an ugly, uncomfortable chair, trying to suppress a sense of urgency he couldn't put to use. He turned away from the counter and looked for a restroom sign. But he saw something much more revitalizing.

Mig had turned a corner at the end of the hall and was striding, then jogging toward him. They caught each other by the shoulders.

"Where were you?" Jess studied Mig's face for signs of distress. "They won't let me see the kid. I'm going out of my goddamn mind."

Tragedy wasn't spelled out on Mig's face. He looked tired and maybe concerned, but not grief-stricken. "Let's go outside," he said. "I need some fresh air."

Jim Bonner came storming through the ER doors just then,

looking as if he intended to take hostages. The skin between his brows had pulled into an arrowhead of furrows.

When he stopped in front of Mig and Jess, his demeanor changed. He lightly laid one hand on Jess's shoulder and one on Mig's. "Dylan, thank you," he said earnestly, then turned to Jess. "Where is he?"

"Still being treated, I guess," Jess said. "They wouldn't let me see him." He gestured toward the reception desk. "Talk to that lady behind the counter. You swing more weight than I do. We'll be outside."

With a curt nod, the old man went to confront Ms. Chasen.

MIG

IT SUCKED to see Jesse looking the way he did. And it sucked to see him under these circumstances.

But it was wonderful to see him at all.

"I was with Red," Mig said as they left that necessary but intimidating place. "He wanted me to be there, so they let me stay for a little while. I told him you and your dad were coming. I think it made him feel better."

"Why didn't you mention that to the old man?"

"He would've asked me questions, and I didn't want to get anything wrong. I just don't know enough about what's going on."

They stopped on one side of the walkway outside the entrance.

"Is Red okay?" Jess stared at Mig with wide, faintly bloodshot eyes. Sucked to see those scarlet threads. Wonderful to see that rich and beautiful jade-green.

"Yeah, pretty much. The worst of it's over."

"How do you know?"

"The doctor told me." Mig managed a smile. "Since I'm Red's brother."

A corner of Jess's mouth ticked, but a smile never formed. "You talked to a real MD?"

"I think so, but I didn't ask or nothin'. I was focused on Red."

Mig was glad they'd kept Jess out of there. The kid was getting fed oxygen through a mask and God-knew-what through an IV apparatus. Hell, he was glad Jess hadn't been around for the first part of this nightmare, when those fiery blotches had first appeared on Red's skin and he'd started to itch, and then had begun to curl up because his stomach hurt, and then wheezed as he struggled to draw air. At least the antihistamines had helped a little. That was what the nurse at the first-aid station had told Mig.

"I was so worried," Jess said in a wavering voice.

His face crumpled and his knees went soft, buckling slightly. Mig didn't have to think about what to do. Reflexively, he caught up Jess in his arms and held him. Jess returned the clutch. Fuck what anybody thought. They were at a freakin' hospital, and when a person you cared about needed comforting in a place like this, you gave it your all.

For that matter, if Jess had needed a hug anywhere, Mig would've given it his all.

He was sick of fighting his feelings.

CHAPTER 13

HOLDING Mig and being held by him felt right, perfectly right, as if their bodies had been formed precisely to fit together. Every message sent by Jess's nerves to his brain—and sent further, deeper, to wherever the rightness or wrongness of touch was registered—affirmed the perfection of their fit. He didn't want to let Mig go. And a pants dance, as Red would've put it, had nothing to do with this desire to hold on.

"I'm sorry." Jess tried to muffle his crying against Mig's skin, cool from the hospital's air conditioning and faintly redolent of sugar and machinery. His lips grazed the spot, although he hadn't intended them to. Or maybe he had.

"Don't be sorry. Okay? Don't be."

"I'm probably"—Jess hiccupped—"embarrassing the shit out of you."

"You're not."

Jess sniffed up whatever snot he could. Drenching the shoulder of Mig's T-shirt was bad enough; he didn't want to wipe his nose on it. But, goddammit, all the built-up tension was gushing out of him, along with a torrent of regret over slapping Red, along with shame over last week's clandestine, hundred-dollar blowjob, along with hurt and bewilderment over Mig's recent distance... and Jess couldn't stanch the flow.

He took a couple of calming breaths. "Man, I'm losing it."

"You're entitled, Jesse. I understand."

"That kid might be a royal pain the ass sometimes, but—" And, fuck, here it came again. "He's… been trying… so hard."

"To do what?" Mig's voice was so gentle, it only made matters worse.

Jess swallowed. "Accept me."

"You mean…."

"Yeah. Being gay. In his own screwy way, he's been trying harder than most adults would."

"Red's a good kid," Mig murmured, smoothing Jess's hair with his hand and ruffling it with his breath. "He'll be all right. You believe that, don't you? *I* believe it. In a day or two he'll be fine."

Sniffling, Jess nodded into the smooth, comforting curve between Mig's neck and shoulder, a secret place he hoped no one else had visited. He raised his face and nodded again, his hair catching on Mig's. The gentle friction felt good, like another kind of caress.

"When we leave here, would you like to go somewhere and talk?" Mig asked. "Or just hang out?"

They slowly eased apart.

"Yeah, I'd like that."

Mig pulled something from his pocket—a handkerchief. He lifted it so Jess could see it. "I think you need this. It's clean."

Jess gave him a weak smile as a memory surfaced. "You still carry a snot rag around?" Grateful, he took it from Mig's hand and wiped his eyes and face.

Mig smiled too. "Comes in handy. Don't you think?"

"I remember how your ma wouldn't let you leave the house without one."

"That was mostly because of my allergies. And I remember all the shit you guys gave me about it."

"I'm sorry."

"You don't have to apologize. That was years ago."

Jess blew his nose as he realized he'd been doing a whole lot of apologizing lately. And it was justified. "I'm just sorry for giving you shit. Ever. About anything." He hesitated, wondering what to do with the handkerchief, then tucked it in his own pocket. "I'll take this home and throw it in the wash." Jess wasn't just being courteous. If he ever needed an excuse to see Mig, he now had one.

They sat on one of the granite benches flanking the walkway.

Jess pulled out the hankie and again blew his nose. "So, who'd you go to the fair with?"

"I was supposed to meet a couple of guys from work. We were planning on catching the demo derby. On my way over here, I called one of them and told him I couldn't make it."

Jess kept watching Mig. "Straight guys?"

"Yeah, of course. That's all there are at Lancer's."

"Ugly ones?"

Mig lowered his head and chuckled softly. "You bet, 'possum-ugly. Even if they went gay for me, I wouldn't want 'em."

Rolling his head back, Jess scrubbed at his face and laughed. "Oh God." He threaded his fingers through his hair, since he hadn't brought a comb, and quickly grew serious. "I'm really glad you're here."

Mig nodded. "So am I."

They stared at their laps. Mig toyed with his fingers.

"I miss spending time with you," Jess said softly. "And I don't mean just because of the—"

The lobby doors hissed open. Jess's father came out of the

119

building much more sedately than he'd entered it. Actually, he looked exhausted. His tension level must have been amped up even higher than Jess's, and he certainly hadn't allowed himself a release through tears.

He stopped in front of the bench. If he noticed Jess had been crying, he didn't let on.

"They're going to admit him and keep him under observation for a couple of days, just in case there's a late-phase reaction. At least they haven't inserted a breathing tube. Not yet, anyway." The old man put his hands over his face for a moment, then flung them down. "Oh *Christ*, why didn't he have a 'Pen with him?"

Jess thought the answer was fairly obvious. "Because he forgot to grab one. Because he's a fifteen-year-old bubble-brain who was all jazzed up about going out with his buds and maybe getting to see Umfy Randall puke."

"Which he did," Mig said. "At least Red's day had a highlight."

The old man shook his head and pursed in a smile.

"Just don't let him watch any more of those *Jackass* shows," Jess advised.

The old man glanced at the ER doors. "Well, I gotta get back in there. You two can leave if you want to. Red's pretty wrung out. He needs rest more than company."

"You sure?" Jess asked.

"Yeah, just go. I'll probably stay the night if they let me, but I'll give you a call in any case." The old man turned to Mig. "I don't know how to thank you, Dylan. You came through like a real hero. I owe you."

Mig blushed crimson. "You don't owe me anything, Mr. Bonner. I only did what anybody else would've done."

"I don't think so," Jess murmured, laying a hand on Mig's

thigh. He got up from the bench before Mig could react.

"See you two later." The old man headed back inside.

Mig got up.

"Let's go to my place," Jess said. "Nobody's there." He all but held his breath.

Mig paused, smoothed his jeans. He looked less uncertain than Jess would have expected. "Okay."

Oh boy.

CHAPTER 14

GRIMACING, Mig eyed the pile of spaghetti on the center island, its sauce darkening and crusting over, its exposed noodles beginning to dehydrate. "We keep *our* leftovers in the refrigerator."

The alarming note now lay beside the heap, its bottom edge soggy with sauce. The old man had apparently tossed it there. Jess lifted the paper and showed it to Mig. "See? Better than a lit-up billboard."

"Ah. Good idea. Nasty looking but effective."

Jess grabbed the kitchen waste bin from under the sink and, reluctantly using his bare hands, scooped the spaghetti on top of the rest of the garbage. After washing himself, he noticed a lone noodle lying in a squiggle on the butcher block. He lifted it and wiped down the surface beneath.

As the pasta hung there, held aloft by Jess's thumb and forefinger, he paused and stared at it. Mig watched with obvious puzzlement as Jess draped the strand over his palm and let it dangle on either side of his upraised hand.

He touched the middle of the length, the part that rested in his hand. "Sunrise Street," he said. He touched one end. "You." He touched the other end. "Me." He looked at Mig. "Is that how you see us now? Is that why you wanted to avoid me?"

Mig's gaze lowered from Jess's face to his hand. "This reminds me of Tomby's little demonstration."

"You didn't answer my question. Do you see me moving in one direction and you moving in another? Do you think we're too far apart now?"

Mig's brows pulled together, and he swallowed. "I don't know, Jesse."

Carefully, Jess placed the noodle back on the butcher block and made a circle. The two ends not only touched but looked seamlessly connected. A rise of fresh emotion threatened to clog his throat. He got rid of it—the physical feeling, anyway—and summoned his voice. "As long as you're here, and we're alone, I need to tell you some things." Extra moisture had gathered in his eyes, and he waited for it to subside before glancing at Mig. "Is that all right?"

Mig nodded.

Jess stared at the pasta loop, at its nearly invisible juncture, and suddenly understood the zero knot. "Just give me a minute," he whispered, because he didn't know quite how to articulate the realization that came with his understanding. He didn't want to give that realization either too much credence or too little.

"I let an older dude blow me at the Faire," he said. "I took money for it. And it's been making me sick ever since."

Mig's brow contracted. "Why are you telling me this?"

"Because a lot of things that've happened lately have made me see other things more clearly." Fuck. Now he was talking in riddles. Jess winced against his words, briefly squeezing his eyes shut. "You know those old storefront awnings you see sometimes in movies, the striped canvas kind that have to be cranked up and down?"

"Yeah," Mig said tentatively.

"Well, the shit that's happened… each event has been like a turn of one of those cranks. When you and I have been together, and I came out to Red, and Bran seduced me, and you rejected me, and I gave in to that guy at the Faire, and Red got sick, and all kinds of other little things in between…." Jess glanced up. He'd been staring

123

at that spaghetti circle, trying to fashion some kind of speech, and he hadn't bothered to see if Mig was even following him.

Mig was. At least, he seemed to be. He nodded once, encouraging Jess to go on.

"All that stuff," Jess said, "each turn of the crank, raised the awning further. And I can see truths I didn't see before. They have to do with this." Jess tapped a finger at the edge of the pasta loop. "Not just my dick and other guys' dicks and getting my rocks off because someone thinks I'm easy; not just a bunch of isolated fucks and sucks with dead air in between." Another glance at Mig, and Jess leaned over the island, his elbows landing on the butcher block with a thud. He dropped his head to his upraised hands. Shit, for a college-bound guy, he wasn't too articulate.

Fingers skimmed the outsides of his elbows. Jess lifted his head. Mig was leaning over the island, watching him, touching him. Those brown eyes didn't say, *What the fuck are you talking about?* They said, *I really appreciate you making this effort.* They might've even said a lot more than that.

Jess lowered his forearms and aligned them with Mig's, skin against skin. The parallel lengths of their arms bracketed the improvised zero knot, pulled from a pile of spaghetti that had once been the center of a family dinner, then used to alert a loving father to a crisis involving his son. Jess stared at the simple circle, his thoughts spinning around it, before he lifted his gaze to Mig's face.

"I want you," he said. "There's no one else I want nearly as much. You're my best friend and my best fantasy and my—" He was going to say "freedom," but he didn't know why. It made no sense. And if he didn't know what it meant, Mig surely wouldn't. "Oh shit, Dylan, I don't know what I'm saying anymore, except I wish you'd give us a chance."

"To be like *that*?" Mig inclined his head toward the pasta loop.

"Yes. Exactly. To be like that. To *believe* we can be like that."

They tenderly moved their fingertips over each other's skin.

A playful smile tugged at Mig's lips. "You want us to be boyfriends?"

Jess stood up, reluctantly breaking their contact. "Yes, I want us to be boyfriends," he said with mock defensiveness. He walked around the island. "Should we shake on it?"

"You can't touch me until I get a ring." Mig was grinning now, a joyful sight.

"The scales will always tip in favor of what enriches your life. That's the thing you'll end up choosing."

Jess could barely force his eyes away from Mig. His scales had tipped; he'd made his choice. Ginger had been right.

He jerked a thumb at the lone strand of spaghetti. "There's your ring."

Mig glanced at it, maybe considering. He nodded almost imperceptibly. "Okay." He stepped toward Jess and kissed him on the mouth, carefully, placing his lips perfectly over Jess's lips, pressing them down neither too timidly nor too aggressively. "Okay." His second kiss carried more ardor, and Jess couldn't help but respond.

Stubble sanded skin this time, and tongues connected, but Mig still seemed intent on taking it slow. The feel of those kisses, the soft pressure and bristly poke, tingled through Jess. Slow arousal was *so* much finer than rocketing to the summit.

"I do want you," he murmured against Mig's mouth. It tasted fruity. They both must've hoped for *some* physical closeness, because they'd both chewed gum on the drive back here. It was kind of sweet, Jess thought as his mouth sprinkled cinnamon on the fruit.

The affectionate kisses continued, like samples doled out in a grocery store. *Here's a hint of what I feel for you. Here's a hint of my desire.*

"I don't want this to be only about sex," Jess said.

"I don't either." Mig kissed along Jess's jaw line. "It's never been only about sex for me."

"Really?" Jess backed Mig up to the kitchen table and gently forced him to lie down on it. He crawled half on top of Mig and began kissing his face, his throat. He ran a hand along the inside and underside of Mig's upraised thigh, careful to avoid the concentration of heat at his crotch. Restraint wasn't easy. The hint had become a promise.

"Really." Breathing hard, Mig clamped Jess's face between his hands and lifted his head for another kiss. "I've been... crushing on you... since we were... twelve, dude." He had to slip his words between the sealing of their lips, the wrestling of their tongues.

Jess boosted himself up. The confession was a surprise. "*Really?*"

"Yeah, really. Why do you think I've been pushing you away? I was scared, man."

Jess slid off the table. Mig followed. Once standing, they both rearranged their cargo, which had suddenly become bulkier.

Son of a bitch, Jess thought. He hadn't realized the power he'd had over Mig, enough power to cause him some hurt. He hadn't realized how long he'd had that power.

But now they were equal. Now Mig had power too.

"I didn't know." Jess sounded as stunned as he felt.

"Well, it's the truth."

And it *was* scary, now that Jess thought about it. When you let someone into your heart, they could do a lot of damage. Sometimes without even realizing it.

"If it makes you feel any better, it looks like we're in the same boat now." Fuck it, Jess concluded. No risk, no reward. He ran his hands through Mig's hair, down the front of his chest, around to the top slope of his ass. "I know we're trying to be all noble about this, but... we can still have sex in our boat, can't we?"

Mig laughed. "It would be a damn frustrating ride if we didn't." He dropped a hand to Jess's crotch and lightly massaged the cargo.

Oh yes, this was what Jess wanted. Nobody's touch ignited him quite the way Mig's did. He yanked Mig's shirt over his head and pulled off his own shirt. Their bodies instantly melded. Jess fingered Mig's nipples, then his own. The feel of them rubbing together, and the sound of Mig's throaty purr, turned his legs into gummy candy.

As their hips automatically pushed forward, Mig said hoarsely, "Can we take a shower? Like now?"

"Sure." Jess kissed him. Their lips were even damper and hotter than their bodies. "We'd better. We're dirty boys."

THEY both came well before they got clean, and when the loofah mitt and body wash were put to work, they came again. It was so glorious Jess could've stayed in the shower stall forever and just kept coming until he melted and swirled down the drain. He wasn't sure what he murmured as he slid his tongue around Mig's neck and chest, as he slid his boner around Mig's cock and sac and ass, but he guessed it was ridiculously raunchy as well as romantic, because that was how he felt.

They almost fucked. They did some tentative poking and probing but never went through with the deed—the first time, because Mig had a sudden orgasm; the second, because they seemed to agree through some weird telepathy that they had to go easy with this phase, had to take their time and do it right.

And, Jess figured, if he and Mig had anything, aside from their euphoria, it was time. They were young and strong and crazy about each other, and all those facts put time at their service. After they finally got out of the shower and toweled each other dry, and as they dashed around the house snapping their towels at each other's bare ass, the phone rang and gave them even more time.

Jess's dad said he'd be staying overnight at the hospital. "Red hasn't taken a turn for the worse," he assured Jess. "He seems much

127

better. But it'll put his mind at ease as well as mine if I'm here. If you want to invite Dylan to stay over, go ahead."

If I want *to?* Jess thought, breaking into a grin the size of Cape Cod and victoriously punching a fist through the air. When he got off the phone and relayed the invitation, Mig got on the phone and informed his parents he'd be spending the night at the Bonners'. The two of them tumbled gleefully onto the couch and rolled around like otters.

Affection laced with desire quickly slowed their movements. Their hands moved more deliberately. Their lips came together and lingered. Jess crawled up the length of Mig's naked body to nuzzle his hair and nibble his ear, then slowly moved back down again, his erection leaving a delicate, glistening trail down the center of Mig's chest and abdomen.

Of course they got excited again. Of course they took care of each other again. These inevitabilities thrilled Jess as much as another development, also inevitable. He didn't want to think about *that* one, though. Not yet. It was serious stuff, too serious for a summer day so brilliant it could coax a responsive joy from two young men. So he didn't mention it. Instead, he and Mig cooked bratwurst and hotdogs and sweet corn on the grill to sate the lesser of their appetites, and Jess let that weightier inevitability withdraw to a warm corner of his heart.

After their supper, he and Mig sat outside on lawn chairs, sipping beers and talking and laughing with easy compatibility. They made no declarations or promises. *Don't want to jinx this*, Jess told himself more than once. The late-August sun sank behind trees and roofs and privacy fences. As its light softened toward old gold, a hint of pink in its patina, Jess reached for Mig's hand. Their fingers intertwined in the glow.

"Tell me when you're ready for bed," Jess murmured, trying to tamp down the anticipation in his voice.

The last bloom of daylight fell away from their linked hands.

"I'm ready now," Mig said.

MIG

HE WAS glad, when Jess finally entered him with halting care, that he hadn't let anyone do this before. Jess seemed glad too. They were able to laugh together and considerately direct and reassure each other and finally make all the wild noises and crazy statements they didn't want to bother holding in. "Ohgodohgodohgod," Jess kept whispering, and Mig could only let out whimpering groans. They rocked in concert, then changed positions, then let a new rhythm capture them. It felt right and natural, all of it, every small move… and finally felt so freaking fabulous Mig could barely stand the pleasure. The prostate gland, he thought, was an anatomical wonder.

After sleeping for several hours, they seemed to awaken simultaneously. They switched giver and receiver roles to find out what best suited them. Although each position had its advantages, they decided, they had distinct personal preferences. Mig admitted to a keener thrill when he was the bottom. (Based on the images that always ran through his mind when he beat off, he'd more or less anticipated that conclusion.) Jess said he felt more excitement when he was the top.

Mig used to worry about "doing it right." But doing it right, he realized, was all about caring enough to take your time and be sensitive to your partner's needs. And, damn, how it paid off. His and Jess's awkward, cautious start had led to a symphony of stimulation and satisfaction. And it wasn't strictly physical.

Around four a.m., as they began their third and final round of lovemaking for the night, Mig asked Jess to turn him on with words as well as with his mouth and hands. Jess was good with words. Mig thought it would be the perfect welding of Jess Bonner with Jess Westry's titillating pulp paperback.

They lay side by side after Jess turned on the nightstand lamp. The sheets, rumpled and askew, looked like the face of a ninety-year-old man with a bad attitude and trouble keeping food in his mouth. But to Mig they were so beautiful the bed could've been a table set in paradise.

Jess lightly traced the lines of Mig's hair and face, neck and shoulders. He talked in a low, husky voice and symbolically kept Mig trapped with the leg he'd slung over Mig's legs.

"I see leather cuffs around your wrists, and chains on the cuffs. You're secured to a pole, your arms above your head. They aren't stretched tight—your elbows are bent—but you can't get free. I come up behind you and slowly run my hands over your body. I'm turned on by its contours and the feel of your skin. It's warm and a little damp but silky smooth, so damned taut over your muscles. You squirm beneath my touch. You want me to fuck you. I tell you that you have to hump the pole first. You have to twine a leg around it and push your cock against the metal until your cock is as hard as the metal. I play with your nipples while you're pushing and sliding and writhing against the pole. I slide my hard dick against the small of your back and finger your asshole. You want to come now, but you can't let yourself; I won't fuck you if you come before I'm inside you."

Mig could see it, practically feel it. The words filled him with a prickly fever. "I'll do anything you want," he whispered.

Jess paused. He petted Mig's hair and let his hand rest on it as he kissed Mig's temple. His touch had gentled. When he spoke, the gruffness was gone from his voice. "I want you to believe in us. That's what I want."

This time they didn't come as quickly. But when they did, their climaxes seemed to roll out of and through each other, and they clung together to keep the current going.

Mig fell asleep thinking about Jess's request. *"I want you to believe in us."*

He'd never responded to it.

CHAPTER 15

THE washing machine was grumbling away, cleaning bedding and clothing and Mig's handkerchief, when the old man finally got home at 10:38 Sunday morning. Jess and Mig jumped apart on the couch as soon as they heard the laborious grind of the garage door lifting. They hadn't been doing anything except reclining against each other as they watched a movie, but two pals being that cozy wouldn't have looked quite right. Not to Jim Bonner, anyway.

"Did you two have a nice evening?" he asked, peering around the corner into the living room. He disappeared again briefly as he hung up his keys.

Jess got up to meet him. "Nothing special," he said, "but it helped to have company. I think I would've gone a little crazy if I'd had to sit here alone."

The old man clapped him on the back and managed a tired smile. "Well, we can all relax now. I'll be bringing Red home tomorrow morning."

"Have you talked to Mom?"

His dad's answer was muted and curt. "Yeah. She said she'll be calling Red."

"Do you think that's a good idea?"

"I don't know, Jesse. But there's not much we can do about it."

The kid was the one who'd suffered most when Jill Bonner had split. It figured, of course, since he was the youngest and therefore the most vulnerable. And he'd been caught in the crosscurrents of adolescence at the time, which made him act out enough to land him in counseling for a few months. Of the three Bonner boys, Red had been closest to their mother.

Too fucking bad she'd never appreciated that fact. Worse that she lived in Tennessee now and rarely came to visit. But since her departure, the four Bonner men had pulled closer and closer together until the space left by her absence had all but disappeared. Only when she called, which reminded them all of her former place in the home, did a sliver of that gap reappear. Thank goodness it sealed back up pretty quickly. Even Red no longer missed her too much.

The old man peered around Jess's shoulder. "Hi, Dylan. Has Jesse been a good host?"

Mig got up from the couch. "Good enough for me, Mr. Bonner."

Suddenly Jess was all smiles inside, wondering how Mig would've answered if he could've spoken his mind.

"I hope he fed you well." The old man approached Mig.

"Can't complain. Especially now that he's washing my clothes too."

The old man shook his hand. "It's the least you deserve," he said warmly. When he saw the rise of color in Mig's face, he turned away. He probably didn't want to embarrass Mig any more than he'd already done.

Jess's heart swelled for his father. He usually took this considerate, unassuming man for granted, but he now seemed a lot less inclined to take *anybody* for granted.

"Well, boys," the old man said, "if you'll excuse me, I really need to take a nap. Spending the night in a hospital isn't exactly like spending the night in a four-star hotel."

"We'll be quiet," Jess said, and Mig immediately reached for the remote to turn down the TV's volume, although it hadn't been that high to begin with. "Maybe we'll go visit the kid today. Or I will." Sheesh, he was already thinking of him and Mig as inseparable. He had to stop doing that. Even boyfriends needed breathing room.

As the old man ambled down the hallway, Jess realized he'd have to 'fess up soon. With each passing day his life felt more like a deception. Now it also felt like a betrayal of his feelings for Mig.

That mention of his mother, whose life seemed to epitomize deception and betrayal, had only put an edge on his conviction.

Jess walked up to Mig and slipped an arm around his waist. When Mig, obviously a little jumpy, gave him an anxious look, Jess erased it with a kiss. "Relax," he whispered.

All Mig did was exhale, releasing his tension. "It's hard to," he whispered back.

He wasn't ready yet. It was difficult to gauge when or under what circumstances he would be ready, and that put a bit of a crimp in Jess's determination to come out. How could he do it without any reference to Dylan Finch?

"If you're going to the hospital," Mig said, "I'd like to come too. Maybe we can pick something up for Red on the way. But let's just wait for my clothes to dry so I don't have to wear yours."

Jess quickly agreed. Red might've been recovering from anaphylaxis, but he would certainly be alert enough by now to notice Mig wearing Jess's clothes. And to make some comment guaranteed to set Mig's face aflame.

CHAPTER 16

"I MET with an adviser on Monday," Bran said as Jess finished filling the dishwasher.

"Was it worth the trip?"

"Eh, I don't know, although he *was* kind of hot in a geeky way. But I hauled more stuff to my apartment, too, so it wasn't a totally wasted trip."

Jess wiped down the table as Bran talked. The kitchen clock told him it was 6:23. He took a few steps into the living room. The old man was still in the shower. Buds in ears and player in hand, and phone within easy reach on the coffee table, Red was stretched out on the couch, where he'd been holding court since his return from the hospital yesterday morning. "I'm still weak," he'd said when Jess had called him out for being a diva. "Not too weak to suck attention," Jess had answered. Dad would probably indulge the kid for another day or so and then put an end to his career in drama.

Tied to the kid's big toe was the *Get Well* balloon Jess and Mig had brought him on Sunday. He'd been doodling on it in multicolored felt-tip pens, covering its surface with cartoon drawings depicting a fanciful version of his "Attack by the Mutant Vampire Bees." Occasionally, depending on his level of boredom or inspiration, Red would sit up, grab the balloon, and add another panel to his story. The kid was actually a pretty good artist. Whenever he spoke of his future, a vision that rarely extended

135

beyond a few days, he talked about being a comic book and graphic novel illustrator.

His phone still at his ear, Jess wandered back into the kitchen and took a seat at the table.

"So classes begin Friday," Bran went on, "which is really stupid, since it's the start of Labor Day weekend."

"Shit, don't remind me. The Faire's gonna be a madhouse. Everybody's on duty, including the weekday crew."

"Yeah, I figured. That's why I haven't moved into my new place yet."

Although Jess hadn't been paying very close attention to Bran—he'd been thinking, as usual, of Mig, of their upcoming pre-bedtime phone conversation and the hours Mig might be able to spend with him at the Faire this weekend—he was focused enough to pick up on that last statement.

"What do you mean?" he asked with a frown. "What does the Ren Faire have to do with you and your apartment?"

A sigh came through the phone. "I'd planned on moving in there last Saturday and paying to sublet through the end of August, which would've given me a week to fuck around on campus before classes started. But when I realized you'd be busy Labor Day weekend, I decided to stay here for most of the week."

The explanation shed no light. Jess's frown only deepened. "I still don't get it."

"You're not very quick on the uptake these days, are you?" Bran's wry chuckle quickly died away. "I'd like to see you, Jess. Lately we haven't seen much of each other, and there's some shit that's sort of... unresolved between us. So, can we get together like tonight or tomorrow? I'll be going back to Madison on Thursday, then coming back for part of the weekend. Only, you'll be working."

Fuck, Jess mouthed, dropping his head to his hand. His first impulse was to say, *You'll be back here plenty. What's the rush?* But that would've been rude. They'd been friends for an awfully long time, this summer's events notwithstanding, and if Jess's recent epiphanies had taught him anything, it was that you didn't take the people in your life for granted. Moreover, Bran did have a point. Issues had been piling up between them and needed to be cleared away—even if a resolution meant the end of their friendship.

Either way, Jess realized, he'd feel relieved.

"Yeah, okay," he said, and quickly added, "Want to meet at the park?" No way did he want to feel trapped in Bran's basement again. Or stuck out at Driftwood Point. Veterans Park was right in town. "I want to be outdoors as much as possible before the weather starts to turn."

"I can dig it," Bran said, although Jess heard disappointment in his voice. Bran apparently felt more in control on his own turf, but that was precisely why Jess didn't want to meet him there.

VETERANS PARK had Norman Rockwell pretensions: a largely unobstructed view of the lake; a central gazebo in white, lavender, and sea-foam green, prettied up with gingerbread and large enough to accommodate a small band; a generic bronze plaque, set into a granite boulder within a flower bed, that memorialized all Cold Harbor residents who'd served in every U.S. war; the requisite scattering of full-crowned trees and picnic tables and barbecue grills on metal poles anchored in cement.

Jess sat on the gazebo steps and took off his shoes and socks. He felt like curling his toes into the perfect carpeting of grass, something he didn't often get to do. Sitting beneath a shade tree would've suited him better, but that was what he and Mig had done at Driftwood Point. Bran wasn't worthy of such comfortable closeness.

A white-and-gray glob of seagull poop landed just inches beyond Jess's left foot. Most residents of Cold Harbor got shat upon at some time or another, and the surfaces in Veterans Park had to be hosed down on a fairly regular basis. Living in a lakeside town came with certain inconveniences.

Forearms on knees, Jess glanced to his right at the small parking lot. "Come on," he whispered. "Let's get this over with." He caught a whiff of smoldering charcoal and fish cooked with butter and onions from a grill far at his back. Two middle-aged couples had settled in at one of the picnic tables. The only people in Jess's line of sight were either on the recreational boat docks or the lakeshore path.

When the breeze shifted, the odors of diesel fuel and summer lake briefly replaced the more tantalizing aromas of an outdoor dinner.

A muted *thunk*—a car door closing—caught Jess's attention. He again glanced to his right. And there Bran was, sleek and golden in the sinking sun. He looked more preppie than hipster today. Maybe the change was accidental. Or maybe he was intentionally remaking himself for college. He might've even been thinking about rushing a fraternity. Whether gay, bi, straight, or dickless, Brandon Nygaard would make the quintessential frat boy.

Jess stood and waved to get his attention. He hadn't seen Bran—except once, in passing, at the Harbor Mart—since he'd literally been caught with his pants down in the Nygaards' spare bedroom. (The image of Mig standing in the doorway still made him shudder.) But he *had* received a couple of e-mail messages. In the first, Bran had apologized, sort of, for the bad timing of his invitations to Jess and Mig: "*sry but i wsnt thinkin. just wanted u to come over asap & didnt consider the possability mig would show up.*" Jess had dashed off what he'd hoped was a dismissive reply: "*it's over and done with. forget about it, k?.*" In his follow-up message, Bran had essentially issued another invitation: "*thx. bn thinkin bout u a lot Jess & rly want to finish what we started, or mbe start somethin new.*" Jess had put off answering that one, and before he could come up with an appropriate response, other external and internal developments had demanded his attention.

The fundamental fact of the matter was that Brandon Nygaard had begun to give him the willies, and he couldn't quite figure out why. Bran wasn't stalking him. Bran had always been a bit arrogant and controlling. Nothing about him was any different, really, and the only aspect of their relationship that had changed was Bran's level of interest in Jess: it seemed to have intensified in recent months. But even that didn't mean much. Bran's attempt at seduction was likely a result of the "Cold Harbor Factor." There weren't a lot of guys in town who liked having sex with other guys. And Jess (if he said so himself) wasn't bad looking.

Without bothering to be discreet, Bran eyed him. "Hey, Jesse." His trademark smirk emerged with the greeting.

"Bran."

They clapped their right hands together and leaned into a hug. Jess quickly pulled back.

"Why are you sitting *here*?"

"Felt like it." Jess pointed at the white blot on the lawn and smiled. "It also helps to have a roof over your head in this part of town." He waited to see on which step Bran would park himself before he sat down again.

Instead of taking a seat, Bran reached into one of his pockets. The shorts he wore were disturbingly similar to the ones whatshisname, Dave, had been wearing at the Ren Faire.

He handed Jess a sheet of paper. "Before I forget, here's my address in Madison. You know you're welcome to come down anytime, especially when you start looking for your own place. And if you can't find affordable housing—"

"Joel has a buddy there who'll be helping me out," Jess broke in before Bran could make his offer. And Jess knew an offer was coming. He could see it in Bran's eyes.

"Okay. Whatever. I'll be coming back here pretty regularly, so one way or another we'll still be able to get together." Bran's tightly knit confidence seemed to have loosened a little.

He finally sat down. Jess, still standing, almost let the paper slip from his fingers like a piece of trash. He folded it as if it meant something to him and slipped it into a pocket, then sat a couple of steps above Bran. He didn't want to sit next to him or below him. Those positions could have invited unwanted contact.

Still, Bran managed to rest a hand on Jess's knee. And immediately thereafter, as if that casual, proprietary touch was the starting point of a preordained process, Bran went into a rambling reminiscence about their years of acquaintance. He concluded it with a question Jess didn't understand.

"Did you get my flowers, by the way?"

"What flowers? I never got any flowers."

"The e-card. Did you get it?"

Jess's mouth fell open. Holy shit, his secret admirer. "That was from...?"

Bran nodded. "I wanted to give you something to think about. Maybe dream about." After brushing something off his leg, he gave Jess an earnest, piercing look. "I'm gonna lay it on the line, Jesse. I've missed seeing you. I want us to be closer." Another pause, and his look deepened toward soulful. "Please, stay with me tonight."

Jess felt sick at heart. He didn't want to deal with this, not when a friend was involved. Rejecting a stranger was one thing—it didn't require much diplomacy and the episode was easily forgotten—but someone he grew up with?

Cringing inside, he said what he had to say. "I can't, Bran."

"Why? Tomby won't be there. Nobody will be there but us." He smiled up at Jess. "No interruptions this time. I promise. Just you and me and whatever you—"

"I said I can't." *Chill. Don't snap at him.* Jess made a conscious effort to ease his tone, to relax his facial muscles. "I'm seeing someone. That's why."

Bran regarded him for a moment. "Someone," he repeated flatly.

140

"Yes."

"Male or female?" An arch tone had replaced the flatness. Bran's smirk underscored the archness.

"I think you know," Jess murmured. He'd never revealed to Bran that he was gay, not bi, but the truth must've been obvious for a while.

"I think I know too," Bran said. "In fact, I know I know. What I can't figure out is why we never talked about it."

Jess had nothing to say. There was no point in trying to explain why he'd never brought up the subject. He didn't know *how* to explain.

"So," Bran said, "did you meet him at the Faire? 'Cause there aren't a whole lot of 'someones' in this town who qualify as dates for you."

"What does it matter where I met him? He means something to me, and I'm pretty sure I mean something to him, and I'm not going to fuck that up."

"What's with the 'means something' shit? You just started seeing some guy and you're already...?" Bran looked nonplussed, with an undercurrent of annoyance. "What are you saying exactly?"

"He's important to me. Okay?" *Chill, dude.* "That's what I'm saying. I don't want to lose him."

"He'd never have to know. For chrissake, there are plenty of people in relationships who stray to play once in a while. And besides, maybe you mean something to *me* too. Maybe you're overlooking a good thing that's right under your nose, Jesse. Hasn't that even occurred to you?"

Oh, man.... "Yeah, it has. So I stopped overlooking him. Now we have a good thing going, and I'm not about to jeopardize it."

Bran stood up and faced Jess. He was turning this into a confrontation, which was exactly what Jess had been trying to avoid. "What if it doesn't last?" he challenged. "What are you going to have to show for all your noble intentions, huh? All that 'I'm determined to be faithful' bullshit? You could end up with *nothing*, Jesse. Nothing but missed opportunities."

"Then so be it." Bravely, Jess met Bran's gaze. "There are some risks worth taking. Haven't you realized that yet?"

"Don't talk down to me, man."

"I'm not talking down to you. I'm just trying to tell you what this is about for me. I figured you might understand."

Bran hooked his thumbs into the waistband of his shorts and stared at the bottom step. He pushed his sole against the riser, leaned forward, leaned back. His mouth, compressed with displeasure, tightened and relaxed with each movement of his body. It weirded Jess out; he couldn't interpret this silent language.

Finally, Bran stopped his rhythmic swaying. "Okay," he said to the ground. After a few seconds, he looked up at Jess. "Okay. I'm not gonna beg. But if you ever change your mind, you know where to find me."

Was he really offering to be Jess's lover-in-waiting? Jess didn't know whether to nod or say thanks or tell Bran not to hold his breath. Shit, this was crazy. A sexual invitation wouldn't have surprised him, but *this*? He was flabbergasted.

"Hey...." Jess stuck out his fist and mustered a smile. "Friends?"

Bran hesitated for a beat before bumping his knuckles against Jess's.

"So, you're leaving on Thursday?" Jess asked.

"Yeah. I haven't decided yet if I'm coming back for Labor Day weekend or not." After a flicker of a glance at Jess, Bran added, "Maybe I'll pop in at the Faire."

Oh shit. No-no-no. "You'd hate it. Trust me. I wouldn't go near that place if I didn't work there. Every holiday weekend is a screaming clusterfuck. You can hardly move without running into somebody."

Bran shrugged. "It's just something to think about." He looked over his shoulder for no apparent reason. "Well, I suppose I'll go home and tie up some loose ends. Maybe I'll see you sometime in the next week."

As he headed for the parking lot, Jess called out, "Bet you'll forget all about the Harbor once you get settled in Madtown. You're gonna meet a whole lot of interesting new people."

Turning to face him, Bran walked backward for a few steps. "Maybe."

When he was safely out of sight, Jess rested his forehead on the heels of his hands and let out a long breath of what-the-fuck… and of relief.

CHAPTER 17

THE spray of broken glass winked from the dirt. Cursing softly, Jess dropped to a crouch and laid down his "shit stabber," a pole with a spike on the end that he used for spearing trash. Couldn't spear glass, though, so he began scooping up the shards with a sieve and then dropping them into a crude-looking sack he wore slung over one shoulder. The strap crossed his chest, which made the garbage-filled sack hang at his side. Thank goodness he was off the main path. If he hadn't been, the herd of Faire visitors would've probably knocked him to his knees or onto his ass.

Mission accomplished, he stood and reattached the sieve to his belt, where a few other tools of his trade dangled. This weekend Jess's "trade" was garbage cleanup—or whatever dumbass faux-Renaissance term the Faire used for that job. Although there were plenty of receptacles for throwaways, people could be lazy pigs.

His vision of humanity improved considerably when he looked up. Leaning against a tree, water bottle in hand and smile on face, was Dylan Edward Finch, Esquire. Jess beamed. Mig strolled up to him and stood close. When their eyes met, Jess felt a thrill that had more facets than a brilliant-cut diamond.

"Are you all sweaty and gritty?" Mig asked in a chocolate voice.

"Mm-hm. And overheated. Is that enough to drive you away?"

"Nope. Drive me crazy maybe." Mig ran his fingers under the strap that angled across Jess's chest. "Which means it's enough to make me help you so we can get sweaty and dirty together… then find someplace private."

Maybe, Jess thought, Mig being here *wasn't* such a good idea. "You really need to keep your hands and your plans to yourself," he murmured.

"Why's that?"

"Because you're already changing my silhouette in embarrassing ways." Oh fuck, Jess wanted to kiss him. Do more than kiss him. Mig's eyes glimmered and his hair gleamed and his smooth, browned skin looked good enough to eat. Or at least lick vigorously.

"I like changing your silhouette," Mig said, his smile a little wider. "Makes me feel like a magician."

Damn, they were shameless. Jess loved it.

"You really want to help me?" He handed Mig the shit stabber. "Here. You can play with *this* pole."

Mig lifted it and eyed the spike. "Ouch. That's the best you can do?"

"For now."

Side by side, they began their leisurely stroll around the Faire. They didn't have much catching up to do, since the made a habit of dropping by each other's house or talking on the phone every evening, but their silences were warm and companionable, and anything but empty.

"You think Bran might actually show up here?" Mig asked. He poked at a paper cup.

Jess grabbed it off the spike and dropped it into the sack. He'd told Mig about his awkward farewell meeting with Bran, although he'd downplayed the drama. "I don't know. You'd think he'd want to keep his ass in Madison, especially with the price of gas being what it is."

Mig exhaled audibly. Whenever he did that, something was bothering him. As Jess took the pole from his hand and impaled a balled-up napkin, Mig said, "Y'know, Jesse, you can do what you want with whoever. It ain't like… it isn't like I expect you to stop being interested in other people."

Jess stopped.

After continuing on for a few steps, Mig turned and walked back to him. "What's the matter?"

The stream of visitors parted and flowed around them. One inattentive kid no more than five bumped into Jess's garbage sack. After steadying him and giving his parents a reassuring smile, Jess hustled Mig off the path near the falconer's station.

"You don't care?" he asked, hurt and incredulous. "You think we should keep playing with other guys?"

Blinking, Mig glanced away. It was harder to detect his blushes as his face grew ruddier from the sun.

"Mig?" Jess gripped his arm. "Tell me. Are we still in, like, 'anything goes' mode? Is that what you want?"

They'd never talked about it. Jess had simply assumed that as of last weekend, their relationship had undergone that cataclysmic shift from fooling around to fidelity.

Finally, Mig met his stare. "No," he said softly, shaking his head. "I just… I didn't know what you expected, so I didn't want to get all possessive and shit. Just because we're closer now doesn't mean I have a right to—"

"Stop. It isn't about rights. It's about what *is* right."

"It's also about making promises you maybe can't keep."

Brows pinched together, Jess leaned forward by an inch or two. "What do you mean? Are you saying you can't trust me? Or yourself?"

Mig briefly closed his eyes. "Fuck. Now I'm making it worse."

"Jesse!"

Jess looked toward the falconer's station. Miles Renarin, the peregrine's handler, was waving him over. Rex sat, head hooded, on Miles's leather-clad arm.

"Shit," Jess hissed without moving his lips. He waved in acknowledgement before again turning toward Mig. "Just wait while I take care of this. Okay?"

Mig nodded and sank to the grass.

"Would you mind cleaning up this crap?" Miles asked, nodding toward the heap of bird doo and the two dead rodents that lay beneath Rex's perch.

The poop Jess didn't mind—it was nothing compared with the reeking mounds of slop left by horses—but those mangled carcasses, already attracting flies, grossed him out.

"My audience is squeamish about the realities of raptors," Miles said in his condescending way, as if his audience were all idiots.

"Well," Jess said as he set to work, "raptors must be squeamish about the realities of people, or Rex wouldn't be sitting there like a sub with feathers."

Miles scowled. "I beg your pardon?"

"Never mind." With a few muffled plops, Rex's leavings landed in the trash sack. "Don't bother to thank me," Jess said under his breath as he hurried to rejoin Mig.

He lowered himself to the patch of shaded grass where Mig sat and made sure their knees touched. "Okay, listen. Here's how I see it. Or how I feel it. Or whatever. I think about you all the time. I fantasize about being with you. And it isn't only the physical stuff I'm stuck on. I'll admit I don't have any experience in the boyfriend department, but considering the track my mind's been on, I can safely assume we've turned a corner, or at least I have, and where we're going or I'm going isn't a place where other guys can go with us or with me. And that spells 'exclusive'."

"You're not alone, Jesse."

"Huh?"

"You keep switching between I and we and me and us." Mig's forehead crimped. "What are those words called?"

Jess's forehead wrinkled in response. "What are you talking about?"

"Those words. I, me, we, us. What are they called again?"

"Pronouns. Why the fuck are we discussing parts of speech?"

Mig chuckled, obviously at Jess's exasperation. "I'm just trying to tell you that you're not alone. I feel the same way. So stick with the 'we' and 'us'."

"Yeah?"

"Yeah."

"But… what were you implying about promises, making promises that can't be kept or something?"

The question sobered Mig. "Just remember that it could all change after January. Or even before, for that matter." He reached for Jess, then pulled his hand back and self-consciously picked at the frayed edges of a patch on his jeans. "We have to be realistic about this, Jesse. We're still young."

Jess felt his mood alter, a change as palpable as an eruption of hives. He knew what Mig was getting at. And he knew Mig was right. A relationship between two eighteen-year-olds, especially two guys, didn't exactly come with built-in stabilizers—especially when one would be moving away in several months.

For now, though, he was head-over-heels in *something*, and he was determined not to cast aside his blissful contentment. It was worth preserving, even temporarily, and Mig deserved his respect.

Jess slid his right hand along the ground and tenderly touched the fingers of Mig's left, nestled among the shoots of grass. When Mig looked up at him, those brown eyes were so full of feeling Jess couldn't imagine *ever* letting him go.

"That doesn't mean we can't be truly together as long as we're together," Jess said. "If it's okay with you."

Mig moved his fingers in response to Jess's touch. Their hands subtly made love within the shelter of the grass. "Yeah. I'd like that."

The spell that seemed to have wound around them was difficult to break, but Jess did have to get back to work. As he rose to his feet, he gripped Mig's hand more firmly and helped him up.

"Come on. I want you to meet my friend Ginger. Then maybe we can… take a break."

Mig

He woke up Sunday morning thinking about returning to the Faire. Or rather, debating with himself about going back. On the affirmative side was spending time with Jess. Of course. But there were too many points on the negative side to ignore. He didn't want to seem too clingy, and he didn't want Jess to get into trouble for spending another shift with a friend in tow. Jess had dozens of coworkers in addition to a few supervisors, and some of them were bound to notice Mig's continual presence.

Still, Jess would've welcomed him. Mig was sure of that. They were wild about each other, and it was almost enough to make Mig say, *Fuck what the rest of the world thinks*.

Almost.

Jess counted on having this job for another two months. He needed the money for school. If Mig played a part in getting Jess fired, he'd never forgive himself.

Standing at the kitchen sink, he vacantly looked out the window. His father and two friends were putting up a new utility shed in the backyard.

Okay, it was settled. He'd go skateboarding along the lakeshore and leave Jess alone to do his job.

When his cell phone sang out, his heart leapt. Maybe Jess *wanted* him to come to the Faire. Maybe Jess was even expecting him.

"Migman, how've you been?"

"Bran?" It didn't seem possible.

"Yeah. I'm only in town for the weekend. Going back to Madison tomorrow afternoon. Hey, I got some people together for a little party up on Beacon Hill. Some of us might even camp there overnight. Want to come?"

"Uh... wow, this is sudden." Mig went to the fridge and poured himself another glass of orange juice. "Who's going to be there?"

"Just some people I haven't seen much this summer." Bran sounded strange. Wired. "You've been sort of MIA lately, so I figured I'd ask you too. I don't want to cut all ties, you know." He laughed sharply. "My moorings in the Harbor. Know what I mean?"

"I guess."

"So, you coming? BYO, not that you have to. There'll be plenty to eat and drink and... whatever. Good shit too."

"What time?" Mig glanced at the clock.

"Oh, say midafternoon. Hold on."

Leaning on the sink, Mig considered the invitation as Bran muffled the phone and talked to somebody who was with him. Yeah, getting stupid on Beacon Hill, or watching other people get stupid, would be a lot more entertaining than sitting at home. This was the last holiday weekend before winter, for shit's sake, and the person he most wanted to enjoy it with was working. He'd still talk to Jess this evening, but Jess would be dead tired. So it wouldn't matter if Mig was dead tired too.

"Hi, Mig! We miss you!"

He abruptly straightened, as if that voice had called him to attention. "Hi, Tomby."

"You coming to our end-of-summer blowout?"

"Yeah, I might drop by."

"Cool. See you later!" After several seconds of disjointed background conversation, Bran's phone disconnected.

As Mig was putting his juice glass in the dishwasher, his mother breezed into the kitchen.

"Have to make lunch for the crew," she said like the perfectly happy housewife she was. "So what's on your itinerary for today?"

"Just got invited to a thing on Beacon Hill." Mig pulled off his ballcap and stirred his hair.

Mom looked over her shoulder as she rummaged through a cupboard. "A 'thing'?"

"Kind of a get-together. Picnic, camp-out, I don't know. Just a bunch of guys and girls from school."

When his mother turned to look at him, her delight was out of all proportion to Mig's news. "Oh, Dylan, *that's* nice." She began pulling things out of the cupboard: brightly patterned paper plates and matching cups, plastic flatware. "It's good for you to be with your friends. For a while you were spending too much time alone, and lately you've been too focused on Jess Bonner."

Frowning, Mig rested his butt against the sink. "What's wrong with Jess Bonner?"

"Nothing. He's a bright young man." She shrugged one shoulder. "Has a strange mother, but nobody can fault him for that."

"No. Nobody can." Mig couldn't control the irritation in his voice. Or the defiance.

He knew damned well that regardless of what his parents said, they did judge his acquaintances in large part through their families. Not going to church, not being sociable enough or active in the community, not having a "respectable" job, not presenting a certain appearance through car and clothing and house were all black marks in the Finch Book of Worth. He was sick of it. And sick of his peers avoiding him because of it.

"Then what *is* the problem with Jess?" Mig asked. Crossing his arms over his chest, he waited for his mother's answer. His face felt like a slab of stone.

She finally turned away from the bank of cupboards and curled her hands over the edge of the granite countertop. "Dylan, a boy your age either spends his free time with a circle of friends or with the girl he's dating. You don't do either. I mean, I understand having a best buddy, but not to the exclusion of having a girlfriend or doing things with a group. It just isn't natural."

Her last statement was like a shower of ice cubes. *It just isn't natural.* Mig's whole life seemed to be contained in that sentence. No wonder he'd always been shy and withdrawn, loved reading and model-building and executing perfect welds. No wonder he'd usually preferred those solitary activities to other people's company. The way he'd always *wanted* to live "just wasn't natural."

Being an only child, a state he'd always hated, had only contributed to his isolation. He had no siblings to deflect attention from him, none to sympathize with him.

Mig pursed his lips and lowered his eyes. He couldn't stand the way his mother was looking at him—with a lack of understanding so deep it seemed like a bottomless dark well. For the umpteenth time, he wondered if he'd been adopted.

"Mom," he said, standing up from the sink, "I'll be getting my own place soon. Then you won't have to worry about how I'm living my life. Okay?"

She tried on a tender smile. "We'll never stop worrying."

"I'm not a bad guy. Just remember that."

"I never said—"

"Just remember that." Mig headed for the hall, for the stairway that would take him to the sanctuary of his room.

When the *fuck* would he have the 'nads to tell them who and what he was? And that he was in love with crazy Mrs. Bonner's son?

153

CHAPTER 18

IT WAS the best of times. It was the worst of times.

"What're you talking about, Mig?" Jess pressed the phone to his face. He could hear the words just fine, but they made no sense. He needed some sense to come through. "Arrested for what?"

It was…

"I'm not sure. Something to do with sexual assault of a minor. I don't know what's going on, Jess."

His voice, oh Christ, his voice.

… the worst of times.

"What minor?"

"Tomby, I think."

Jess's dad, his expression somber, wrapped an arm around his son's shoulders. "What's wrong?" he whispered.

Jess waved him away. "Tomby? That's bullshit! What happened?"

"I don't have time to talk about it. My parents are getting a lawyer. I'll put you on my visitors list, okay? And I'll call again when I can. Okay? Write to me or something."

"Yeah, yeah, okay, whatever, but what the fuck—?"

The line went dead.

Jess glared at the receiver in stark disbelief, as if it had just bitten his cheek, then angrily hung it up. He fell into a chair at the kitchen table and hard-scrubbed his hands over his face.

"What on earth is going on?" his dad asked. He too took a seat.

Then Red was there, his expression mirroring the old man's. He suddenly looked ten years older.

"Mig is…." Jess's voice faltered and got stuck in his throat, stuck in some knotted mass of confusion and fear and impotent outrage. He was on the verge of tears. "He's in jail. It sounds serious."

"What?" The old man was incredulous.

"Fuckin' Tomby has something to do with it."

"Oh man," Red groaned. He briefly dropped his head to his folded arms.

"I need to know what's going on. I have to talk to her. And the Finches." Jess pushed back from the table.

Before he could make another move, his father gripped his arm. "Jesse, no. Don't go off half-cocked. You could make matters a lot worse for Dylan. And yourself."

"I have to *do* something!" Jess yelled.

"There's nothing you can do but wait. I'm sure the Finches are taking care of it in every way they can. If it'll make you feel better, call the county jail tomorrow and find out when their visiting times are and how you can write to Dylan. But he might even be out by tomorrow."

His father's advice was sound, but it didn't alleviate Jess's fear and frustration. "Fuck it," he said, bolting up from the table and heading for his room. "This is insane."

He'd no sooner dropped onto his bed than a timorous knock sounded at his door.

"Leave me alone."

The door cracked open. Red's face appeared. "Jesse? Are you okay?"

Numbly, Jess shook his head no.

Red crept inside and carefully closed the door behind him. He paused, waiting to see how he'd be received. When Jess didn't explode and lunge at him, he padded over to the bed and, still in slow motion, sat beside Jess.

Of course, his deferential silence didn't last. "Mig is your boyfriend, isn't he," the kid said, making it a statement rather than a question. "It kind of just happened, didn't it."

His voice was as kind as when he'd talked to and petted Clifford just before they fell asleep together each night. The sound of it nearly made Jess crumble into tears. But he battened down his emotions and merely answered, "Yes," although he wasn't sure Red could hear him. The word was little more than a puff of air.

"He's a good choice," the kid said conclusively.

That did it. Jess's shoulders started to hitch. He made himself put the brakes on the breakdown. This was some kind of mistake, after all, some super-twisted misunderstanding, and Mig would be sprung in no time. His parents had some sway in this town and had the money to give it a voice.

Yet, behind all his self-directed assurances, Jess felt like a terrified little boy trying to be brave. Mired in confusion, he felt utterly helpless.

Red saved him from spinning out of control by saying, "You know what? I think Dad might've figured it out."

"Figured what out?"

"That you... like Mig as more than a BFF."

Jess jerked his head over to the right to look at the kid. "Did you—?"

"No, dude. I didn't say nothin'." He affected a look of umbrage. "Jeez, give me *some* credit. And Dad too, for that matter."

"So what makes you think he knows?"

"I just got that feeling from the way he was looking at you. Like he's been kind of fiddling around with a lock for a long time, trying to get it open but only in a half-assed way, 'cause he wasn't even sure it was *worth* getting open. Then all of a sudden, *shazzam*, the tumblers just fell into place." Red's face scrunched with uncertainty. "Or whatever happens inside of locks."

Jess dropped his head to his hands. "Great." Just what he needed right now, on top of this other shit—his dad having an epiphany about his sexual orientation.

Red patted Jess's leg. "I wouldn't worry about it, dude."

"Of course you wouldn't."

There was another knock at the door. Jess groaned into his palms. His father came into the room.

"Red, go find something to do."

The kid acted perfectly composed, as if he and the old man were equals. Jess knew *that* wouldn't last. "I already found something to do," Red told him. "I'm doing it right now."

Dad's face tightened. "Jared, don't play games with me. Find something to do outside this room."

"Call your girlfriend," Jess said wearily.

Red got off the bed with a great show of effort, as if he were struggling to overcome gravity. "Which girlfriend? The last one who dumped me or the next one who'll dump me?"

"Then call Umfy. He can't afford to dump anybody."

When the kid finally made it out the door, the old man took his place on Jess's bed. He just sat there for a while, forearms resting on thighs, and tapped his fingertips together. Jess felt no anxiety, no defensiveness. He was empty, as passively expectant as a bored security guard.

"Is there anything you'd like to talk to me about?" the old man finally asked.

"Nothing you don't already know."

The finger-tapping picked up speed for a moment then abruptly ceased. "*Are* you gay, Jesse?"

Jess met his father's gaze. He wasn't going to make the most monumental admission of his life with shamefully lowered eyes. Besides, Mig deserved his courage. And pride.

"Yes."

His dad merely nodded.

Seconds ticked by in silence.

"When did you figure it out?" Jess asked.

"Today." The old man chuckled faintly. "Well, let's just say I swung from mostly unsure to mostly sure. I've really been getting the strong impression lately that Dylan is pretty special to you."

Jess hesitated, nodded.

Something thumped against the outside of the bedroom door.

"Jared!" the old man barked.

The word *crap*, quiet but emphatic, came from the hallway; then, a few carpet-muffled footsteps. Red's door whispered open and clicked shut. Smiling, Jess wagged his head.

Dad took a deep breath and let it out as he hunched forward again. "So, you're gay. And you're in a relationship with Dylan Finch."

Speaking these truths seemed to help the old man absorb them, manage them. Jess realized it was a personal kind of magic his father had always practiced. Whenever he learned something that was potentially unsettling, he repeated that information aloud. It somehow made him feel in control of his world.

Jess reinforced the magic, maybe skimmed some off for himself and Mig. "I'm gay. And I'm in a relationship with Dylan."

"You must have strong feelings for him."

"Yup." Jess shoved both hands into his hair and curled over. Tears burned his eyes. "Oh shit, that sounds so drama-queen mushy."

The old man rubbed his back. "Caring about someone is never wrong. And hey, you're only eighteen. Adolescence to adulthood is the Era of Angst in a person's life. You have a license to gush and fret and suffer. Take advantage of it while you can. The time is coming soon enough when you'll be expected to hold everything in and keep a stiff upper lip."

The speech touched Jess. His dad sounded envious of the Era of Angst. And resentful of the Era of Strength and Self-Control. "It must suck," Jess said. Again, he had a sense of what burdens his father had shouldered over the years, how he'd done so with uncomplaining grace.

"Sometimes, yeah."

"The divorce must've been tough."

"Divorces usually are."

Jess angled toward him. "How... how do you know if somebody is right or wrong for you?"

The old man let out one dour laugh, but plenty of irony was packed into it. "Don't you think you're asking the wrong person, Jesse?"

"No. I don't think I am."

His dad hesitated before smiling. He might've thought Jess's faith was misplaced, but it pleased him nonetheless. Modestly, he lowered his eyes. "Well.... First, get to know yourself. And that's not easy, believe me. Then look for a good fit. Gut instinct is part of it. But keeping the blinders off and your eyes wide open is a bigger part. It's kind of like... finding just the right beads to match the ones on your own string." He cocked his head. "Know what I mean?" Groaning, he shook his head. "Damn, I hate metaphors."

Jess laughed. "No, I get it. I do." And he liked it, the image of all those complementary beads strung along the same loop, with just enough variation to make the necklace interesting. Values, priorities, tastes, personality traits. They didn't have to be identical, but they couldn't clash.

"For the record," the old man said, "I think Dylan's a great fit for you."

The words made a lump in Jess's throat. "I do too," he whispered.

The old man got up. Jess followed. His dad cupped the side of his face and looked into his eyes. "I love you, Son. And I have enormous respect for Dylan." Then Jess got the kind of hug he hadn't received from his father in longer than he could remember.

As he hugged back, he let his tears fall.

It was the best of times. Squeezed from the worst of times.

He was determined to make it so.

CHAPTER 19

JESS looked forward to Mig's calls and dreaded Mig's calls. Since phone conversations were likely monitored, the two of them were wary of saying the wrong things; in fact, had no clear idea what constituted the wrong things. The world of criminality, of arrest and incarceration, was alien to both of them. So Mig was overly cautious and circumspect about his case—only told Jess he'd had an initial hearing and was hoping to be out on bail soon. "According to Warburg," he said, referring to his lawyer, "what's holding things up is there's some confusion about what exactly I'm being charged with." When Jess asked what he meant, Mig replied, "I shouldn't say more than that." He gave Jess visitation details, the days and times for which were divided up among the jail's "blocks," and talked a little about what it was like to be there, and continually reiterated his bewilderment about being there.

The best part of those collect calls was hearing Mig's voice. The worst part was hearing Mig's voice. He sounded distracted and depressed. Jess wanted to reach through the phone and hold Mig or, better yet, yank him out of there, but the most he could do was say things like, "I miss you" and "I believe in you" and "I'm sure this'll get straightened out soon." Red even wrote Mig a letter full of groan-worthy jokes, goofy drawings, and heartfelt encouragement. Although Mig was amused by it and seemed deeply appreciative, his reaction had an undertone of humiliation that tore Jess's heart to shreds.

He finally got to see Mig early Friday evening.

Visitors had to check in fifteen minutes prior to the start of the visiting period. Jess was there twenty-six minutes early. He made sure to leave his cell phone in the car and bring nothing with him except his wallet, where all his forms of identification, save for his birth certificate, were stashed. He felt nearly insensate as he stood before the pane of bulletproof glass and presented himself for approval. Then, stomach twisting and nerves tight, he sat in the barebones waiting area and vacantly watched other inmates' friends and relatives dribble in.

The boogeymen of anxiety, fluorescent lights, and sleeplessness tormented him, another ménage made in hell. He couldn't wait to see Mig. He dreaded seeing Mig in this place, under these circumstances. Visions of his lover shuffling toward him in handcuffs and shackles, face gaunt and eyes hollow, sent a shower of acid through Jess's stomach. He kept looking at the institutional clock on the wall, his heart lurching with every precise twitch of the second hand.

And then it was time.

Along with the other visitors, he filed into a narrow room with double rows of cubbyholes, each outfitted with a short countertop and black wall phone, each facing an identical cubbyhole. The two rows were divided down the center by a wall-to-wall sheet of Plexiglas. Heart pattering, he sat in one of two molded plastic chairs. Within seconds, a line of men shambled in at the other side of the barrier. No cuffed wrists and chained ankles, thank goodness, just really ugly jailbird suits.

Suddenly, Mig was before him.

He smiled wanly, and Jess smiled back. They lifted the receivers of their phones.

"Hi," Mig said. He didn't look *too* terrible. A little drawn, maybe, with a hint of ash-gray crescents beneath his eyes. But his hair was soft and clean, and his arms were still tanned, and a wedge of his chest was visible within the neckline of that baggy uniform shirt.

Jess tried to block out the uniform. "Hi. It's so freakin' wonderful to see you again."

Mig blushed, swallowed, looked down. "I know this is maybe asking too much of you, but...." When his eyes again met Jess's, nothing would have been too much. "Please believe I didn't do anything. I shouldn't be here, Jesse. I swear to God. I have no idea why Tomby said whatever she said."

Oh *fuck*, this was maddening. "Of course I believe you. That goes without saying. But can't you give me a better idea of what exactly went on? Please, Mig, can't you? It would help me understand."

"I don't even understand. How can *you* understand? I was there and you weren't, and I still don't understand."

True. All Jess had learned so far—from both Mig and Mig's father, who'd talked to Jess's dad—was that this whole mess had stemmed from some camp-out on Beacon Hill. Mig was certain somebody had slipped him something, but not too much of something, because he'd never felt "completely out of it." Based on Mig's description, it sure as hell sounded to Jess like Ecstasy.

Mig's lawyer had thought so too. However (Attorney Warburg had told the Finches), Ecstasy wasn't specifically targeted in most drug tests, so the theory couldn't be proved or disproved. Mig's piss test had only shown a relatively low level of alcohol.

"All I know," Mig said, "is that I didn't touch her. Not in any kind of 'inappropriate' way. Why would I even want to? I've never wanted to."

"Were people touching *you*?"

Mig hesitated. "Some. A little."

"And it felt good." Jess had done X twice. MDMA's street name was apt. He wasn't much inclined to do it again, though, because he'd since learned about its long-term effects and what other drugs it might be laced with.

163

"Yeah, okay," Mig said. "It felt good. But that doesn't mean *I* did any touching."

"Not even yourself?" Jess had significantly lowered his voice, but the question still seemed to stress Mig out.

"Jesse, I don't want to talk about that here. Besides, what does it have to do with anything?"

So the answer was yes, then. Mig had likely been dosed with X, at least with a little bit of X, and he'd gotten enough of the warm fuzzies to let other people grope him. He'd probably beaten off, or let someone else beat him off, before he fell asleep. He said he'd brought a sleeping bag and crashed for several hours before driving home around 3:00 a.m.

Jess wasn't sure what the jerking-off part had to do with anything, but it seemed it might be important.

"All I can do," Mig went on, "is tell the truth and hope Tomby pulls her head out of her ass and finds her conscience. That's all I can do, Jess. I don't know what possessed her to accuse me of shit. I just can't figure it out. I know for a *fact* I didn't do nothin' to her. Or to anybody."

"So did you tell your lawyer and the DA and whoever the hell else just *why* these charges are so outrageous? Did you tell them you're gay and you have no interest whatsoever in—"

Mig's forehead dipped as he sent a *shhh* through the phone to silence Jess. His eyes slid to the left and right, anxiously scanning for eavesdroppers. "No! Are you crazy?" He hunched farther over the small counter, bringing himself closer to the Plexiglas barrier. "Then everybody'd know," he mumbled. "Family, neighbors, the whole crew at Lancer's, all the customers. I'd be *done*."

Jess gaped at him in disbelief and despair. "And you won't be 'done' if you say nothing? This is serious shit, Mig. She's a freakin' *minor*."

"It'll be okay," Mig said with limp conviction. "I got the

impression from Warburg that she's been changing her story a lot. That combined with her reputation doesn't make her look too good."

"Well… is there any other sort of evidence against you?" First Jess couldn't think of the word he wanted. Then it came to him. "You know, corroborating evidence? Or is this just a she-said and he-said thing?"

Mig licked his lips and looked indecisive. "I shouldn't say anything more. Okay?"

Oh fuck, now what did *that* mean? Jess rested his forehead in his hand. "Mig, listen to me. The fact you're… what I said before, is your greatest defense. Don't you see that? And I could verify—"

"I'll tell you what I see. Making a big hairy announcement to the world wouldn't put me in a very good place. I don't need a defense that's gonna lose me my family and job, Jesse. At least right now I have everybody's support. I'm not gonna be running off to Madison, you know. I gotta live here."

"Why?" The question came out of Jess's mouth as if some force beyond himself had pushed it out. And simultaneously planted the reason for the question in Jess's mind.

Mig looked mystified. "Huh?"

Jess leaned closer to the barrier. "Why *can't* you run off to Madison? With me? We could get a place together. You know damned well you can write your own employment ticket. You're that good at what you do. Christ, Mig, you can't keep letting fear determine how you—" At that point, Jess realized they'd been cut off. The phone line was dead. He had no idea how much or how little Mig had heard.

They stared helplessly at each other. *Call me*, Jess mouthed, and impulsively pressed his fingers to the Plexiglas as he mouthed another phrase: *I love you*. He kept his eyes fixed on Mig as Mig rose, staring at him, and he mouthed the words again, slowly and deliberately. *I… love… you*.

More than anything, he wanted to say it out loud. To Mig, as he held him. And to the world, as he defied it to find fault with what he felt.

The second thing he wanted to do, and ASAP, was find Tomby.

CHAPTER 20

JESS didn't call Tomby on her cell. He didn't want her to know he was looking for her; she surely would have avoided him. So he called her parents' landline, pretending to be a guy from school who wanted to invite her to a birthday party.

She wasn't home on Friday night. Jess tried again on Saturday, pretending he'd lost her cell number. She wasn't home then either.

"Is she somewhere in town?" he'd asked in his best innocently hopeful voice. And it worked. Her mother, who still spoke with a Spanish accent, told him she'd gone biking along the lakeshore.

Jess headed for the paved path, determined to walk up and down the length of it until he ran into Tomby. If that didn't work, he'd camp out in front of her house until he spotted her going in or coming out. Giving up was not an option.

He was about three-quarters of the way to Driftwood Point when he saw her approaching from the opposite direction, pedaling at a leisurely speed. He slowed his steps and pulled his cap farther over his eyes.

When Tomby was nearly upon him, Jess bolted in front of her. She squeezed the brakes. The front wheel of her bike jagged to the right, and she quickly dropped a foot to the ground to steady herself. Jess grabbed the handlebars on each side of their pivot point. He could see Tomby's eyes widen behind her sunglasses.

"Shit, Jess, you almost made me—"

"I want to talk to you. Now."

"Can't you see I'm doing something?"

"I sure the fuck can. I can see you're ruining someone's life. And I want to know why."

The bike wobbled as she tried to wrench the handlebars out of his grip. "Leave me alone."

"Okay, screw the courtesy. You're going to talk to me. And don't try pulling any bullshit. I don't think you want me to start spilling everything I know about you."

When Tomby realized she was powerless, her chin began to quiver. Jess could feel her resentment biting at him. *Tough shit*, he thought. *The power trip stops here.* Big boobs and a big brain did not a goddess make.

"How would you react if your papa were accused of a crime he didn't commit? Huh? How would that affect you, Dominga? And your family?"

The quivering turned to trembling. Something was going to give. She'd either lash out at him and become even more viciously determined to pursue this course, or she'd relent. Jess waited to see which way it would go. In either case, he wasn't going to let up on her.

"Why're you sticking your nose in this?" she asked sullenly.

Jess tightened his hold on the handlebars and leaned forward. "Do you think," he said with quiet ferocity, "it might be because I see you stabbing a friend in the back, somebody who never did anything to hurt you? Do you think it's because I *care* enough not to sit by and watch it *happen*?" On each of his emphasized words, Jess gave her bike a hard shake. And Tomby flinched. "Why?" he asked again in a coarse whisper. He could almost see the sound of it abrading all the burs off her stubborn resolve.

"Let's sit down somewhere," she mumbled.

She steered her bike into the scrubby growth at the side of the path. Jess followed. After about ten feet, she unceremoniously let the bike fall sideways into the vegetation and kept traipsing down the embankment that led to the lakeshore, stepping high to minimize contact with scratchy branches and rash-inducing leaves. Jess simply swept through them. He was wearing jeans. And he was incensed.

Low waves more like ripples lapped indifferently at the sandy shore, nudging at a line of slimy weeds, a couple of dead fish, and scattered bits of flotsam. With a flouncy movement, Tomby dropped to a sit. Drawing her legs up to her chest, she immediately snatched up a water-smoothed, sun-bleached stick and began poking aimlessly at the sand.

Jess sat beside her.

"I know what the zero knot is," he said. "I understand its purity now. And its permanence."

Tomby's poking slowed, but she still wouldn't give Jess the courtesy of looking at him.

"I've learned all about it through my dad and my brothers and Dylan Finch. And I know there are people who exist just to cut up those unbroken loops, or try to, so they can selfishly twist the pieces into uglier knots, destructive ones that suit their own purposes. And when they get sick of those knots, they'll undo them and remake them into other ugly knots. But you can't remake the zero knot—can you, Tomby? You can push and tug at it, curl it up or stretch it out, but it'll always remain what it is, unchanged. It will always be a complete circle."

"Why're you telling me something I already know?" she muttered petulantly.

Jess finally faced her. "Because you *don't* know. Can't you see the zero knot isn't just a mathematical abstraction? Can't you see it has another name? Jesus, you should. You have a family."

Oh yeah, she got it. She was biting at her lower lip and staring intently at nothing, which could only mean an unsettling realization had hit her.

"What's the other name for it?" she asked, barely moving her mouth.

"Love."

Suddenly, Tomby stopped scratching at the sand and jammed the stick into it. "We really weren't like that, were we? The Domino Club, I mean. We were never part of the same loop."

"No, we never were. We only pretended because we all knew we were different somehow. So we tried to be the same kind of different. But we weren't. Nothing truly bound us together."

Thoughtfully, Tomby nodded. "Do you love Mig? Like, romantically?"

The question surprised Jess. He didn't think she was capable of noticing romantic attachment unless it was melodramatically put on display. "Yes," he said, his voice subdued but firm. "I'd do anything for him."

Tomby wiggled the stick with the tip of her forefinger. "I don't think Brandon feels that way about me."

He doesn't give a rat's ass about you, Jess was tempted to say. *Anyway, fuck you and Brandon; let's get back to you and Mig.* But he held off, because Tomby actually seemed to be feeling something, not just analyzing and scheming and congratulating herself on how clever and masterful she was. Her defensiveness hadn't melted away, but it had softened.

She tilted her head to look at him, her face puckered with uncertainty. "What do *you* think?"

"I think you're right."

After a brief pause, she whispered, "Yeah." Squinting against the water's glare, she hugged her shins and set her chin on her knees. "It's *you* he wants, you know. He can't stand it that he hasn't been able to get you. And it really pissed him off when you blew out of his basement that one evening."

Jess's heart beat faster. "What are you telling me?"

Tomby was still, didn't so much as blink. "It was all Bran's idea. He hates the Finches. And he *really* hates Mig."

"Why?" Jess really didn't need an answer from Tomby. He was suddenly, sickeningly aware of the answer. Bran knew about him and Mig. Of course he did.

For starters, Bran had probably seen them making out in his driveway. In and of itself, that incident wouldn't have meant much to him. He would've chalked it up to lack of impulse control fed by horniness. But subsequent bigger clues—Jess blasting out of Bran's basement to go after Mig; Jess confessing to having a boyfriend who'd been "right under his nose"—had given away the whole game.

"He knows you've got something going on with Mig," Tomby said from a vast distance, although she hadn't moved. "He knows you're hung up on Mig, that the two of you are pretty heavily involved. He tried to tell me Mig had done something to him, something outrageous and disrespectful, and he was after some payback. But now"—she abruptly lowered and straightened her legs—"now I see what's really going on."

Jess couldn't imagine the look on his face. He could only feel the ratcheting tension in his forehead and around his eyes and mouth. "He put you up to this because he's jealous? He tried to destroy Mig's life because he's *fucking jealous*?"

"You know it's more than that," Tomby murmured. She'd begun to look genuinely troubled, as if the sheer cold-bloodedness of Bran's motives, and the selfishness of her complicity, had finally smacked her good and hard. "You know how he is when he doesn't get his way."

"No. Apparently I don't." Was this Bran's idea of vengeance? Or was he simply trying to remove what he viewed as an obstacle to his wish fulfillment? Ultimately, it didn't matter. The fucker was a sociopath. "How exactly did he put you up to this? And what exactly have you been telling your new friends at the cop shop?"

Tomby's look of distress deepened. She let out a wavering

sigh. "First he organized that stupid party on Beacon Hill. He doesn't give a crap about those people, not really. He just wanted to set Mig up and get him out of the way."

"Did somebody slip Mig Ecstasy?"

"Yeah, but not even a full cap. Bran knew Mig wasn't much of a druggie and probably didn't have much tolerance. He was afraid of getting busted if Mig had a bad reaction or something. It was still enough to get Mig a little loose, though, you know? So Bran started peeling off his clothes and, like, doing a striptease for Mig, touching himself and touching Mig and shit. But Mig wasn't cool with it. At all. I mean, his body might've been cool with it but his mind wasn't, you know? 'Cause he kept saying shit like, 'Come on, man, stop. There's someone I care about. I don't play anymore. I'm not interested.' But Bran wouldn't stop. He kept workin' Mig and saying shit like, 'Your someone will never have to know.'"

A spasm tightened Jess's stomach. That was the same thing Bran had said to *him* at Veterans Park.

Jess wanted to throw up. What kept his breakfast in his stomach was that he felt spellbound by Tomby's tale, by the ruthless self-interest it implied. He'd encountered that motive before, of course, but he'd never seen it carried to such extremes.

"Bran didn't care if all those other people saw him acting that way?" Jess didn't ask if Mig eventually gave in. That was for Mig to tell him, not anybody else.

"Of course he didn't care," Tomby said. "For one thing, 'those people' already know he's bi. Shit, even his parents know. And for another thing, everybody was too drunk or doped up to care. On top of it all, he's living in Madison now. So there was no reason for him to give a shit about how he looked, especially if he could make Mig look bad."

All true. So true. It was Mig who had everything to lose, not Brandon. "So where do *you* come into it?"

"Well...." Tomby again drew up her legs and dropped her

forehead to her knees for a moment. She took a deep breath. When she continued, she looked even more bothered by the realizations Jess was forcing her to confront. "I think at first Bran was just hoping to get Mig to cheat on you, make him look like he had no willpower and would cave to any guy who came on to him. Bran wanted to trash him in your eyes, in front of witnesses. And out him too, I guess, which would've set up all kinds of hell for him at home and maybe at work. But Mig *didn't* cave. All he did was walk away from it. He opened up his sleeping bag so he could catch some Zs before he drove home."

"But something happened, Tomby. What the fuck happened? And how? And why?"

She crept closer to tears. Jess saw it in her face. Little Miss Know-it-all Badass, who seemed capable of flipping off her own grandmother, was skidding toward being Dominga Martinez again, the good Catholic girl who was only sixteen.

"Bran was working me, too, not just Mig. I think he's been working me for a long time. He said, like, 'Come on, baby, this is a challenge now. We gotta break this uptight son of a bitch. We'll double-team his ass. I think he's thizzin' enough.' So just as Mig was crawling into his sleeping bag, me and Bran sort of crawled in with him and worked him some more." Tomby slid Jess a guilt-tinged glance.

MIG

DEAR Jess,

I just want you to know I been thinking about our talk. How I cant keep hiding behind a lie, always afrade what other people will think if I be myself. Cold Harbor is not the world and my parents cant drive my life thru the world like it was in the trunk of there car.

I want to do rite by me and second to that I want to do rite by you.

I love you Jesse. I love you with all my heart. Even if we dont last, you helped make me strong.

XO

Dylan (Mig)

CHAPTER 21

"AND?" Jess sounded shrill. He had to guard against that. Even though apprehension made his gut ache, he had to be in control. He *had* to be.

"I don't want to talk about it, Jesse." With that, Tomby broke. Strangled whimpers came from her throat.

It was a relief, however temporary. She was the one who'd cracked instead of Jess. She hadn't answered his question, but that was all right. Jess didn't want to hear the sordid details anyway. He was already inferring too much. All he wanted to hear now was that she was willing to recant and make things right.

Tomby sniffled and swiped her nose across her upraised knees. "I hate myself. Bran's a fucking manipulator. He doesn't give a crap about me. He probably never did. Now I got *this* shit on my shoulders, and he's gone, and he didn't even get his pinkie dirty."

Maybe her remorse had only to do with allowing herself to be used by Bran. Maybe she finally realized she'd been chumped and left holding the bag while he trundled off to Madison and promptly forgot about her. It was hard to say whether a genuine conscience played a part in Tomby's sorrow.

But none of that mattered. Only the ultimate result mattered.

Jess swiveled on the sand so he could face her. "Listen, little girl. You need to go to the DA or whatever counselor type they assign to underage victims, and you need to tell the truth. First thing Monday morning. Tell them all the stuff you told me, and all the stuff you *didn't* tell me, and make it clear Dylan Finch wasn't guilty of a goddamned thing except minding his own business and keeping his hands to himself."

Tomby's face crinkled like a raisin. "I *can't*, Jesse," she whined miserably. "They'll nail me for something. Filing a false report or whatever. Maybe worse. And how are people going to look at me? Especially Bran? He'd be *furious* if I dragged him into this!"

Jess's first impulse was to yell, *I don't give a fuck!* But he instantly knew he had to exercise some finesse. He must try to think like the psychologist he aspired to be.

Okay, Tomby's concerns were valid... to her. If Jess had any hope of persuading her to come clean, those concerns had to be addressed and somehow minimized. There also seemed to be a flicker of conscience behind her confession, and he had to fan that spark into flame. She needed to feel the kind of guilt that could singe her soul.

Jess started out by saying, "I understand." Tomby looked a little shocked at first, then dubious. But she was intrigued enough to keep listening. Jess adopted a tone that he hoped would garner her trust—calm and rational yet empathetic. "It sucks that Bran made you his pawn. Jerking somebody's chain always sucks. But I know how it can happen. When you're in love with someone, or think you are, you're not seeing clearly. And you'll do anything to make that person love you back. That doesn't mean you're weak or stupid, just human."

Tomby's impenetrably dark eyes examined his face for signs of a con. She wouldn't allow herself to get too soft too soon. Her gullibility with Bran had been humiliating enough. She wouldn't let Jess get one over on her too.

"Has it ever happened to you?" she asked warily.

"No. Mig's the first person I've ever loved. So I've been lucky." *Remind her. Drive it home.* "He's the opposite of Bran—sweet and considerate and honest. But you should know that by now."

Tomby lowered her eyes. After a brief hesitation, she nodded. Moisture twinkled on her lashes. "I still don't want to bring Brandon into it. I know what a mean prick he can be. *Now* I know."

As much as Jess wanted to see Bran go down, he had to be mindful of Tomby's concerns. If he pushed her to do something she resisted doing, he could lose any chance of getting through to her. "Yeah, he can obviously be a lot more vindictive than we realized," Jess said, trying to balance condemnation of Bran with sympathy for Tomby, although he felt precious little sympathy for her. He did appreciate Tomby's dilemma, though. The girl had a large, loving family. They, at least, deserved some protection from any fallout.

"But that means I'd have to take the whole rap," she said, wavering again.

"Maybe not quite. Think about this. You've got your age and gender in your favor. The law bends over backwards to understand young girls and give them a break."

"But I'm not—"

"Just hear me out." Jess took a moment to strategize. "Let them know how sorry you are. *Show* it. Tell them you'd been drinking or doing drugs that night, whatever the case, and because you don't get high very often, it really impaired your judgment. There was a guy there you wanted to impress—you don't have to name him—and you figured that pretending you'd been assaulted would get his attention and sympathy. Then emphasize that Mig is completely innocent, and emphasize again how bad you feel. That would work, Tomby. They're not going to drag a sixteen-year-old girl over the coals for one lapse, especially if she's truly contrite."

Brows drawn, she stared at the shoreline.

Jess dipped toward her face. "You *are* sorry, aren't you?"

Her face folded again, and she made a constricted mewling sound that ended in a very childlike "mm-hm."

She *was* young. Under all that swagger and insouciance, Dominga Martinez was just another insecure teenager who'd idealized somebody not worth idealizing—she'd seen a perfect rosebud where she should've seen a perfect asshole—and, desperate for his approval, had done something incredibly reckless. Adults were capable of the same idiocy. They overlooked or made excuses for the egregious behavior of loved ones, became part of serial-killer fandoms, married imprisoned felons, or stayed married to abusive shitworms.

Jess thought of his dad. Had Jill cheated on Jim? Jess had a feeling she had. Was Natalia really a Russian parasite looking for an American host? Maybe she was. Had it taken or was it taking Jim Bonner a while to figure this stuff out? Yup.

Jess had been mighty shortsighted himself. Brandon Nygaard had sent up plenty of red flags from his rotten core, but Jess had ignored them. Instead he'd chosen to see the charm, the intelligence, the generosity and genial schmooze. So there was more than enough dumb-assery to go around.

"Jesse?"

Tomby's timorous voice jerked him out of his thoughts. "What?"

"Will you ask Mig not to hate me?"

"I can't do that. I can't read your mind to know how sincere you are. Only your actions can make him hate you or not. So if you deal with this as soon as possible, no delays and no excuses, I'm betting Mig will forgive you. A heartfelt apology sure as hell wouldn't hurt either."

"Will you... will you write a letter saying what I just told you?"

"Why?"

Unease of a different sort overcame Tomby, and she picked nervously at the sides of her shoes. "I'm just worried I won't say the right things in the right way. Or I'll freeze up. I'm better with numbers than I am with words. And it's different, you know, talking to those people than talking to you. So this way, I can just hand them your letter and say, 'Here's what really happened. This is what I told my friend Jesse. He wrote it all down 'cause I was afraid of screwing up if I had to explain it to you.' And they'll maybe ask me if your statement is accurate, and all I'll have to come up with is a yes." When she finally looked at Jess, anxiety was written all over her face.

Jess doubted it would be *that* easy—she'd certainly have to provide her own statement and sign it, at the very least—but he understood her desperation for help. It was damned hard, fessing up to a lie. Even for a jaded adult. And Tomby had puked up one whopper of a fabrication that had landed an innocent person in jail. Yeah, she had every reason to be anxious.

"That seems like a weird way to go about it," Jess said, "but I'll do anything that could help get Mig released. You need a ride to the courthouse on Monday?"

"I think I should have my folks take me. Or at least my mother, if my father can't get off work. Don't you think so?"

"Yes, I do. I'm glad you're open to that. I didn't think you would be."

Tomby shrugged. "They're gonna have to know sooner or later what's coming down." A tear leaked from her eye, the one Jess could see. She quickly swiped it away with the side of her hand and stared at the lake.

"Okay, then. I'll stop by your house either this evening or before noon tomorrow and give you the letter you want. Just be there. And, goddammit, don't wimp out on Monday morning."

"I won't. I want this to be over and done with, man. I want to wash my hands of it." She let out a shuddering sigh. "I just hope Bran gets what he's got coming to him."

Jess hoped so too. In fact, he considered delivering that karma himself.

MIG

"I'M SORRY to bother you at home, Mr. Warburg, but there's something I have to tell you. It's a big reason why I wouldn't have done anything... anything improper with Tomby. I mean, Dominga Martinez."

"Oh?" Warburg seemed to be talking around food in his mouth. After a few garbled sounds that could've indicated chewing, swallowing, and wiping with a napkin, the lawyer's voice returned to normal—crisp and nasally. "What is it, Dylan?"

Mig's throat suddenly felt arid. He swallowed hard. "I'd rather not talk about it over the phone. But I don't know if you can get in to see me today."

Warburg chuckled in a smug way. It reminded Mig disconcertingly of Brandon. "Oh, I can pretty much see you any time I need to. But can't this wait until Monday?"

Humility tried sabotaging Mig's resolve. He refused to let it. *Asshole. You wouldn't be trying to blow this off if it was* your *kid who was sitting here.* "No. It can't wait. This is something I ain't told... haven't told anybody. But I should've."

"Hm. Well, I'm sufficiently intrigued to make a call and drive over there. You sure you can't just tell me over the phone?"

Mig glanced around. He was sure. "You'll understand why when you get here."

CHAPTER 22

JESS closed his bedroom door after he'd taped a block-printed DO NOT DISTURB sign to its exterior. Since he rarely did such a thing, he suspected the sign would be taken seriously. He hadn't told his father where he'd gone, and he sure as shit hadn't told Red. Too much uncertainty swaddled his current effort, so there was no point in talking about it. Moreover, he didn't want to waste time and lose focus answering questions or listening to lectures.

Sitting on the bed with his laptop, he got the basics down first. Date, time, and location of his meeting with Tomby. How many years and how well he'd known her. Then he sketched in the framework of what had transpired that day—Tomby's voluntary, often tearful revelation of a lie she'd concocted in the hope of winning an anonymous boy's sympathetic attention. There'd been drugs and alcohol involved, and they'd further clouded her thinking and lowered her inhibitions. Mild-mannered Dylan Finch, who'd been slipped an Ecstasy mickey, had simply been an unwitting player in the girl's scheme. He was the victim, not the perpetrator.

Jess filled in the details. It killed him to have to leave Bran, the string puller, out of the picture, and he had to make an effort not to bring up Mig's sexual orientation.

In some paragraphs Jess got carried away and ended up over his head in his own rhetoric. He realized he had to correct that. Whoever read this wouldn't appreciate tripping over clumps of purple prose, and they might even question his truthfulness. Overstatement always invited skepticism.

So Jess went over what he'd written, highlighting ineffective, irrelevant, or overblown phrases, then went over it again. He reconstructed. He deleted. Although he'd graduated in the top ten percent of his class, and his most recent English teacher, Mr. Przybylewski, had emphasized the importance of revising with a "merciless editor's eye," Jess still wasn't sure where his editor's eye kept itself or how to call it forth. Considering Mig's freedom was at stake, he started second-guessing every other word he put down.

It looked like Tomby would get her letter Sunday morning instead of Saturday evening. Jess hoped her parents would be in church when he delivered it.

Finally, head hurting and eyes crossing, Jess wrapped up his account. *"It was my impression,"* he concluded, *"that Dominga engineered a situation she did not have the maturity to manage. She's deeply sorry, and even asked me to tell Dylan Finch not to hate her. She wants nothing more than to put an end to this whole mess."* He saved the letter, printed it, signed and dated it.

Now that his task was completed, Jess left his room and told his father about the day's events. The old man was appalled to hear how Mig's arrest had come about, but he wasn't exactly shocked. He'd never fully trusted either Bran or Tomby.

Jess didn't have to endure any dire warnings about his involvement. Instead, his dad said, "I'm proud of you. Even if she backs out, we're going to give copies of this account to the Finches and the district attorney. Dylan's been sitting in other people's shit for too long. It's an outrage."

That was the shot of courage Jess needed before his visit to the Martinez house. He felt vindicated.

ON SUNDAY morning around ten thirty, he drove to the old neighborhood. There was only one Catholic church in town, and Jess had learned years ago when Mass was being held based on the increased traffic around the church and the fullness of its parking lot. Given the time, Tomby's parents shouldn't be at home.

Sunrise Street didn't look much different, except that the shade trees had grown a little and a few homes had gotten facelifts. He went to the side door of the Martinez family's spacious colonial and, when Teresa answered, asked for Tomby. She came to the door wearing a Japanese-style bathrobe and a towel wrapped around her obviously wet hair. Jess had forgotten what a diminutive girl she was. Without the slutty clothes and heavy makeup and tortured hair, Tomby looked poignantly young and delicate.

"You still good with this?" Jess asked, handing her a manila envelope.

All the sass seemed to have been washed out of her and sent down the shower drain. She nodded slightly, holding the towel in place with one hand. "I'm actually looking forward to it. Kind of. It's like I've had this big ol' grizzly bear on my back with its claws digging into my shoulders. I want it off me."

"Have you told your folks yet?"

"I'll tell them when they get back. They're always, I don't know, full of a gentle kind of spiritual glow when they get out of church." She shrugged. "It ain't *my* kind of gig, but it works for them."

Jess was about to depart when Tomby said, "Oh, wait." She reached into the pocket of her robe and pulled out what looked like a bracelet, hand-strung with beautifully colored and patterned beads. As she handed it to Jess, her demeanor softened further. Into modesty. "I made this yesterday. I know it can't erase what happened, but it's... like a token. Or whatever. It just means... well, you should know."

Jess studied the bracelet. The nestled beads were all different, their dainty, raised designs made of glass lines and dots meticulously applied to the glass spheres. But they all blended together perfectly. He didn't see a clasp. Whatever juncture there was between the two ends of the string, which might've been fishing line, was invisible. He gave Tomby a quizzical look.

Shyly, she pointed at one bead that was larger than the rest, a pearlescent ball that bore an iridescent heart. The knot must've been concealed within its hole. The two pairs of beads that cozied up to it, one on either side, were uniquely different from the rest.

Because they carried letters. J beside B on one side of the heart; D beside F on the other.

Immediately, Jess's face began to quiver. His eyes burned. Tomby pretended not to notice. She gave him a quick sisterly hug around the waist, murmured, "I'm really, really sorry," and withdrew into the house, easing the door closed behind her.

MIG phoned later that day but was strangely taciturn. "I had a hell of a time getting to use the phone," he said. "Seems everybody in here wants to call like a hundred people on the weekend."

Jess held the bracelet as he listened. His heart wanted to throb out of his chest and through the phone and land in Mig's hands.

He said nothing about Tomby. He didn't want to get Mig's hopes up. As cooperative as she'd been, she was still an unpredictable kid who had a big family to deal with. Anything could make her bail: the psycho-emotional trampoline she was on; pressure from her parents or sisters. And if she had any contact with Brandon—shit, game over.

"You don't seem to have much to say," Jess noted.

"Not right now. But I might have more pretty soon. I just didn't want you to worry about me."

Jess managed a wan smile. "Thanks. I *would've* worried if I hadn't heard from you. But what do you mean by 'more'? Is something happening you should tell me about?"

"Maybe. I'm not sure yet. Stuff grinds to a halt on weekends. Except for these guys' mouths. Man, can they talk. Speaking of which, how's Red doing?"

"He's back in school. And back to his old self."

"Can't keep a good punk down, huh?"

Jess laughed.

"What about your dad?"

"I think he's been a little blue lately. That woman he's been seeing apparently met some other dude and went to Milwaukee with him. Possibly for good. Maybe I'll introduce him to my friend Ginger at the Faire. Or maybe Red and I should join forces and try to find him some prospects on the Internet."

"I vote for hooking him up with Ginger." Mig was silent for a moment. "I'm glad I wasn't forced to jump through all those hoops. I'm really grateful, Jesse."

Jess fingered the centerpiece beads on the bracelet—the initials, the heart. "I am too," he said quietly.

He hadn't bothered trying to find the tiny knot that held the circle together. He preferred to believe there was no knot, that the loop had no beginning and no end.

As if the bracelet were capable of some woo-woo mind control, Jess said without forethought, "I love you, Dylan."

And like magic, the words came back to him, with a slight alteration. "I love you too, Jesse."

They'd done it. They'd joined the ends together. Nothing, nobody would have a chance to sever their loop.

MONDAY'S mail debunked the magic of the bracelet. A short letter from Mig arrived. The same declaration was contained within it.

Since he didn't have to work that day, and the old man and kid weren't around, and sitting idly at home would've generated enough fretting over Tomby to eat away the lining of his stomach, Jess went shopping.

At Pier 1 Imports outside of Sheboygan, he found a lovely box in which to keep the beaded bracelet and Mig's letter. It had plenty of room for other mementoes. He hoped he'd have as much time with Mig as the box had space. More, really. A lot more.

Jess was definitely in love. Fuck it if he was being a mush pot. He was eighteen. He'd take his dad's advice and work on building his masculine stoicism and fortitude at a later date.

He told himself the same thing when he got home and saw the Cheshire Cat grin on Red's face as the kid relayed a message from Mig.

"He said to tell you he's getting out. Maybe as soon as tomorrow. And he wants you to be there. He'll call again later with the deets."

The kiss Jess planted on Red's face was enough to wash every freckle from the kid's skin.

MIG

HE STOOD just inside the door, staring at the gray sheet of rain that nearly obscured the parking lot, wishing those flashes of lightning were splashes of sunlight. Man, how he longed to feel sun on his face again.

Tuesday afternoon. He'd been in that miserable zoo for just over a week, but it felt like a year. Thank God he'd had the nuts to tell Warburg he was gay and had zero sexual interest in women of any age, shape, or size. Thank God doubly that Tomby had verified his claim by stepping up and calling herself out as a liar.

Mig grudgingly gave her credit for that. He hadn't been told the details of her 180, how it had come down, what exactly she'd said and whom she'd said it to, but at least she'd pulled him off the hook she'd put him on.

Now… now he had to deal with his father. Harry Warburg had definitely dropped the gay bomb on Tom Finch. Mig could tell just by the sound of his father's voice during their recent chats. Dad had never brought it up—he wouldn't do so over a county jail connection—but Mig's little talk with the lawyer had hung over their brief conversations like a glowering troll. Too bad Mom was out of town, stranded in Oklahoma City because of storms. It wasn't that she'd celebrate her son's coming out or clutch him to her bosom and purr, "What matters is that you're happy," but she was the one more likely to stay calm and less likely to reject him.

187

Brushing a hand over the fogged glass, he scanned the vehicles in the lot. His father would be picking him up. But Mig had told Jess approximately when he'd be processed out, so they could at least catch a glimpse of each other.

Oh yeah, he was in love. He couldn't wait to hold Jesse again. Since that wasn't possible in the immediate future, he'd settle for a look. Just one look.

Mig's stomach clenched as soon as his father's Lexus pulled into the parking lot. He shoved the door open and, at the same time, saw Jess's Escort approach from the opposite direction. Jess slid into a parking space that was as far away as possible from Mr. Finch's. He quickly got out of his car and stood beside it, facing the jail entrance.

He and Mig smiled simultaneously when they caught sight of each other. Actually, Jess beamed. As Mig's dad fished around for something in his vehicle, Mig subtly raised a hand in Jess's direction. Jess, who was two rows behind Mr. Finch and therefore not worried about being seen, thrust his arm above his head and waved. Then he blew Mig a kiss. Mig's smile expanded to a grin. He hadn't thought people did stuff like that, except in movies, and it made him feel on top of the world.

Only... the world tilted and tossed him into space when his father finally reemerged from the Lexus. He turned, snapped open an umbrella, and walked toward his son. Mig's expression sobered as he approached not just a ride but a turning point in his life. He tried to keep his peripheral vision trained on Jess. The sight of Jess pumped him with confidence.

"Thank God the truth won out," his dad said while centering the umbrella over their heads. He gave Mig a one-armed hug and a pat on the back.

Yeah, Mig thought. *I second that.*

For the life of him, Mig couldn't absorb anything his father talked about on the ride home. Or he absorbed just enough to give brief responses. Extended silences broke their stunted exchanges.

188

During these, Mig stared vacantly out the window, trying not to anticipate what was surely to come.

His adrenaline level rose as soon as they pulled into the garage.

"All right," his dad said, shaking off the umbrella once they were out of the car, "time to clear up a few things. Grab yourself something to eat if you're hungry. We can talk at the table."

Here it comes. Mig entered the house and pulled a Pepsi from the fridge. Already feeling drained, he flopped down at the kitchen table. He stared longingly at the patio table beyond the sliding glass doors, although its umbrella was folded and rivulets of rainwater streamed steadily down the creases. He just wanted to be outside with Jess again, the two of them alone under the sky.

His dad came in from the attached garage and also got himself a soda before he sat at the table. "Now what's this story you told Harry Warburg?" He affected a chuckle, but it sounded more mean-spirited than mirthful. "You must've been damn desperate to get out of there. But who can blame you?"

Mig took a drink. "It wasn't a story. It was the truth." Suddenly, this man didn't seem very much like his father.

Hazel eyes fixed on Mig, Tom very carefully set down his soda can. "You've got to be pulling my leg. Unless somebody brainwashed you into *thinking* it's the truth." His chuckle had carried over and become more blustery, bouncing his words as he spoke them.

"It's the truth," Mig repeated evenly. "Remember, life is a never-ending process of self-examination."

No laughter now. "Who talked you into this?" Tom, grim-faced, thrust himself farther over the table. "*Who?*"

"Nobody. It's what I am. Have always been. It's *who* I am."

"Bullshit! You're covering for the pervert who poisoned your mind." Tom narrowed his eyes. "Did this happen to you in jail? 'Cause I swear, if some sicko—"

189

"No. Nothing happened to me in jail. I've known for years."

Huffing out a breath, Tom glared. Sometimes, like now, he seemed never to have left the military. His hair was trimmed neatly short, its edges so straight and sharp they threatened to cut into his temples and the back of his neck. Tendons strained above the collar of his golf shirt. Muscles bulged below its sleeves.

Already despairing, Mig shook his head. Trying to explain, even if he knew how, just wasn't going to work.

"Is Jess Bonner behind this?" Tom asked ominously. "Is that why he was here so late that one night? Why you slept over at his house? Why you went to the Renaissance Faire alone on Labor Day weekend?"

It would've been so easy to scream, *Yes! But not in the way you think!* Instead, Mig stared at the table's centerpiece and thought of the steel he worked, how only the right touch applying the correct amount of heat could persuade it to alter its boundaries. He tried to be like the steel. His father had the wrong touch and the wrong degree of heat. Mig wouldn't yield.

"Leave Jess out of this," he said. "It's *my* life we're talking about." He pushed back from the table. Sitting there was making him feel boxed in. "At least I never got anyone pregnant. And never will." The reassurance had a snide undertone Mig couldn't control. His parents had always warned him about getting some girl in trouble. It seemed to rank among their biggest fears. "Wouldn't you say that's one big advantage of being gay?"

"Quit using that sick damn word!"

"What word do you want me to use?" Mig got up, his boundaries still intact. "If you and Mom can't handle this, I'll move out as soon as I get my room packed up. I've been planning on finding my own place anyway." He walked away from the table.

"Dylan!"

Mig took his time stopping and turning.

"We'll forget this conversation ever took place if you just tell me that fag crap was your Get Out of Jail card."

"It was," Mig said. "That's why I'm leaving."

CHAPTER 23

"HEY, Jesse! Your ex-con boyfriend is here!"

Jess bounded out of his bedroom. Damn kid must be psychic in addition to his other aberrations. He'd been standing at one of the narrow windows flanking the front door, as if he'd been expecting somebody.

Sure as shit. Mig, head lowered and shoulders hunched against the rain, was striding toward the stoop.

"Jared, get away from there!" Dad called as he entered the living room from the kitchen.

Jess shoved the kid out of the way and swung the door open.

Mig looked up and smiled, sad but sweet. His dark curls were plastered to his head like gleaming swirls of tar. Water trickled off his face.

"Hi," he said softly. "Did you miss me?"

Jess pulled him inside and into a hug. They clung together, faces buried in the curve of each other's shoulder. Mig's clothes erratically dripped water onto the foyer tiles. Moisture wicked into Jess's shirt and jeans. But beneath the cool, sopping drape of Mig's clothing was Mig's body, hard and warm. His heart thumped against Jess's chest. His breath caressed Jess's neck.

"Yes," Jess finally answered. "Oh hell yes."

They wanted to kiss. At least Jess wanted to kiss Mig, and he sensed the desire was mutual. But they had an audience. Who else but Red reminded them of that?

"Wow," the kid said from the living room, "it's just like the ending to *An Officer and a Gentleman*."

Jess felt Mig's ribcage spasm with suppressed laughter. "Wait for it," he whispered.

"But I can't figure out who's the officer and who's the gentleman. I think Mig is more of a gentleman than Jesse. Don't you?" The kid must've been asking for their father's opinion. And he got it.

"I'll tell you what I think." The old man's voice faded slightly and changed timbre, as if he'd turned away. "I think we need to empty the dishwasher." After a beat he said more loudly, "Jesse, get Dylan some towels and give him dry clothes to change into."

"Not just yet," Jess whispered.

He held Mig's face and kissed him. Petted his slick, wet hair and kissed him. Pushed his hips against the patch of heat below Mig's waist and kissed him more fervidly. Their lips slid as much as their tongues did, but they managed to make enough contact with enough passion to convey what they were feeling.

"I love you," Jess said, just to erase any doubt. He licked a line of water that threaded from Mig's ear to his jaw. "I love you so much." He licked along Mig's eyelashes, catching minute droplets on the tip of his tongue.

Mig alternately moaned in excitement and laughed. They kissed again, more heatedly.

"Come on," Jess said, "let's get you dry. I think we've been given a chance to be alone for a little while."

After Mig pulled off his shoes and left them in the foyer, he and Jess went into the bathroom together. The so-freakin'-wonderful old man kept the punk occupied in the kitchen. Jess stripped off

Mig's clothes and, in the process, went from half hard to fully rigid. He shoved down his own briefs and jeans.

"I'm sorry we can't take too long with this," he said breathlessly against Mig's mouth.

Not that they needed a prolonged engagement.

As they kissed with wild, sloppy abandon, trying to stifle the moans that stuttered in their throats, they groped and frotted to climax in under a minute.

"I'll get you some clothes while you dry off and clean up," Jess said, swiping a damp washcloth over the mingled cream on his own hands and belly. "Oh, Christ, it's so good to see you again."

Mig smiled. "Ditto."

Jess discreetly crept out of the bathroom. His father surely suspected he'd gone in there with Mig, but why be obvious about it? Flaunting the sexual part of their relationship would've been crude and insensitive and disrespectful, even if they were a hetero couple. After grabbing some clothes from his bedroom, Jess went back to the bath, knocked on the door, and slipped the clothing inside.

He wanted to slip himself inside too. He was already getting horny again just thinking about Mig standing there naked.

"I'll be waiting in the hall," he said.

"Okay. I'll be right out."

Jess leaned against the opposite wall, arms crossed over his chest, and smiled in a dreamy but decidedly lecherous way at the closed door. He was so much in love at that moment, and so much in lust, it seemed the rest of his personality had been consumed by those feelings. He envisioned two Pac-Man figures, one pink and one scarlet, scurrying through the maze of his mind, gobbling up dots.

Shit, I've been around Red too long.

When Mig came out, carrying the wet jeans, shirt, and socks he'd shed, it once more occurred to Jess that he didn't exactly look happy.

He took the bundle of clothing from Mig's arms. "Is something wrong? You seem down."

"I'm not. Not really." Mig fidgeted. "On Sunday I, um... told Warburg I was gay, and Warburg of course told my father, and... we just had a little discussion about it."

Jess's face fell. He could well imagine how *that* had gone. "Oh, shit. Are you all right?"

"Yeah. Yeah, I'm fine. Kind of relieved, actually." Mig smiled in a strange way, both proud and sorrowful. "I've moved out. Well, I'll *be* moving out. Until then, I'll have to stay at a motel."

"The fuck," Jess said. "Go have a seat on the couch. We'll talk about this after I throw your clothes in the dryer."

He hurried through the kitchen to the laundry room. The old man and the kid were playing Monopoly at the table.

"Is Dylan all set?" his dad asked.

"Oh, I'm sure he is," Red muttered as he kept his eyes glued to the game board.

"He's relaxing in the living room," Jess said to his dad. "When you're through here, I need to talk to you about something."

"Oh, I'm sure you do."

Jess flicked the kid's game piece, his beloved shoe, off its place on the board, then went about his business.

Red's voice continued to wind from the kitchen as Mig and Jess settled into the couch, and rain continued to patter against windows and walls and roof. Jess didn't turn on the TV. The whole scene was a lot homier without it.

"We'll get this taken care of," Jess said to Mig. "I promise. You can stay here."

"Jesse, I came over to see you, not to ask that you put me up."

"I know."

A piece of commentary from Red sliced into their conversation, although it had nothing to do with them. The kid was still in the kitchen, trying to be the Donald Trump of Cold Harbor.

"I'm not jivin' you, dude."

"Excuse me. It's *Dad*, not *dude*." Dice rattled and spilled.

"Sorry. But seriously, Dad, *queer* is okay. It's like Two-tone doesn't care if he's called an Indian. He says most Indians use the word *Indian*. They put it on their websites and everything. Two-tone says it's mostly educated white dudes who juice their Jockeys—"

Mig snorted.

"—if you don't use *Native American*, which Two-tone says has more syllables than people need to wrap their tongues around. Oh, and speaking of which—"

"Don't even go there," the old man said.

"No! No, I wasn't going *there*. Except in a kind of roundabout way. Meaning I do have a pretty good idea what terms piss gay guys off. So don't sweat my language." Red grumbled out something about Park Place.

"Jared, I break into a sweat every time you open your mouth."

Jess couldn't remember the last time he'd felt so purely content. The night of Mig's sleepover came close, but Red being in the hospital had scratched at the back of Jess's mind that evening. Now, though, Red was in the kitchen, happily running his mouth. Jess and Mig lounged at opposite ends of the couch, smiling into each other's eyes, socked feet sliding over socked feet in a casually seductive way.

"I love it here," Mig said in a muted voice.

The old man strolled back into the living room as Jess and Mig sat up straighter.

"He came out to his father tonight," Jess said immediately. "It didn't go too well."

The old man's forehead crimped with concern. "I can't say I'm surprised. You're more than welcome to stay here, Dylan."

Jess smiled and lifted his eyebrows as if to say, *See? Told you so.*

"Would we have to rename him Jylan?" Red called from the kitchen. "Or Jig? Heh."

Jess craned his neck to see what the kid was doing. The Monopoly game was still sprawled over the table. Now Red moved between the refrigerator and island as he filled a serving tray with sandwich fixings.

The old man sat in his recliner. "I think Red's determined to feed you," he told Mig with a smile.

Laden tray supported by both hands, the kid came into the living room, set the food on the coffee table, and parked his skinny ass between Jess and Mig.

"Go ahead and eat," he told Mig. "My Spidey senses told me you're hungry."

"I can read him like a book," Dad said. He grabbed the remote from the end table and hit the numbers for CNN, but he kept the volume low.

Mig lifted the bag of submarine sandwich rolls. "I'm starved. Thank you."

"Hey, no problem. I'm happy to feed people who save my life." Red reached for the tray. "So you don't feel self-conscious, I'll have a bite with you."

"We just had supper," Jess pointed out.

"Not just."

"Dylan?" Dad said. "I'm serious. You can stay with us as long as you need to."

"You don't have the room, Mr. Bonner." Mig was in the process of assembling a killer sandwich. Jess felt guilty for not offering to feed him. "And I don't want to impose."

The old man smiled reassuringly. "It wouldn't be an imposition. Believe me. I'd love to welcome you into our little circle, as long as you don't mind bunking on the sofa. It pulls out into a queen-size sleeper. A good one."

Jess loved his dad for offering. He loved Red for putting out the food. He loved Mig for just about everything. Life, at that moment, was good.

Except.... He and the other two adults darted sidelong glances at the kid, who'd become the red elephant in the room. Mig and Jess couldn't sleep together because of him. Everybody knew it, probably Red included. Only, his mouth was too full for him to comment on the situation.

"Maybe I should get one of those little efficiencies at the Breakers Motel," Mig said. "Just until I find a place of my own."

"*Our* own," Jess corrected.

He was torn. It would be like a cohabitation practice-run to have Mig staying in the Bonner house, and it would be wonderful to share all the intimate minutiae of daily life with him—breakfast and dinner, household projects, peaceful evenings, the hijinks of Red and the boys. But the lack of privacy would be excruciating. They were young men, not old monks. And they were in the early stages of a pretty intense romance.

Mig looked just as conflicted. At least it wasn't interfering with his appetite. His sandwich was an inch thick and disappearing rapidly.

"I think we should talk about it," Jess said to him.

Mig swallowed and took a drink of the juice Red had also put on the tray. "I think so too."

"Bet you want a love nest," Red said, now that his food had traveled from mouth to stomach.

"Bet you won't be offering any more opinions tonight," Dad said. "Bet you're going to bed after you clean this stuff up."

"The school bus waits for no man," Jess said. "Or twerp."

CHAPTER 24

JESS and Mig retreated to Jess's room when Mig was finished eating. Jess made it clear to the old man that they simply needed to talk. His father didn't look dubious or issue any warnings, and once they were behind the closed door, Mig said with wistful envy, "It's incredible how understanding he is."

"I'm beginning to realize just *how* incredible." As if to validate his dad's trust in him, Jess sat on the bed rather than stretch out and invite cuddling.

Mig sat cross-legged, facing him.

Before they got around to discussing Mig's housing situation, Jess finally told Mig how he'd waylaid Tomby last Saturday and what she'd revealed in the course of their talk. He told Mig about his letter. But he held off bringing out the bracelet. Tomby's betrayal was still fresh, and Mig might resent or at least be suspicious of her gift.

As impressed and grateful as Mig was—and Jess felt profoundly humbled by his reaction—Tomby's revelations about Brandon's role, and his motives, really stuck in Mig's craw.

"So Bran was behind it all," he said bitterly. "I should've known."

"How'd it come down?" Jess asked gently, for neither Mig nor Tomby had related that part. "How'd it go from Bran trying to seduce you to Tomby getting you arrested? All she told me was that

Bran had been 'working' you, and then the two of them... did something after you'd crawled into your sleeping bag."

Mig traced the squares of plaid on the coverlet. He didn't meet Jess's gaze for what seemed like minutes, but his face was rouged with heat. He pulled the knuckle of his forefinger over each eye, rubbed his nose, cleared his throat.

"I hate telling you this," he said in a half-broken voice. "Especially after finding out how much you did for me."

Jess touched Mig's knee. "It's okay. I know what the effects of X can be. I'm not exactly a drug virgin."

Mig nodded but didn't seem reassured.

"Hey, it's not going to change how I feel about you."

Apparently, that assertion was enough.

"They were all over me," Mig mumbled. "I got hard. Then Bran rubbed me off. Maybe they both did. I don't know. I kept my eyes closed. I suppose some of my... some stuff got on Tomby's leg or on her shorts or shirt or something. Maybe Bran even put it there."

Jess stared at him. "Fuck." The revelation sunk in deeper. "*Fuck.*"

"Yeah. 'Oh fuck' was pretty much my reaction too. Warburg, my lawyer, kept making these vague references to DNA evidence, how damning it could be."

Jess rocked backward, hands clamped over his face. "That goddamn conniving bastard Brandon. And then he convinced Tomby to claim that you...." Mouth agape, he shook his head in disgust and disbelief. "I wish she'd told me that part. I would've for sure put it in my letter. I wouldn't have given that prick a pass if I'd known."

"In a way, I was lucky," Mig said. "After Tomby finally coughed up the truth, I found out that the only reason they didn't railroad me was because of how weird she'd been acting. She'd miss appointments, clam up or act really volatile during interviews, change her story. I don't know how Warburg caught wind of that shit, but I suppose every player in the justice system around here knows every other player."

Jess had to take a deep breath after hearing Mig's side of the incident. He wanted to pound the smugness right out of Bran's goddamn face, and he said so.

"It's over now," Mig said quietly. "I don't want to dwell on it. I just want to keep a lot of distance between myself and those two."

"Did you ever tell your father about Bran's part in it?"

"Shit, no. He'd have gone ballistic. And I'd *never* tell him what you found out from Tomby, that Bran was the mastermind behind the whole thing. He'd probably start some civil suit or something, and I'd have to testify, and it would turn into a big ugly scandal that would spread all over town. You know the Nygaards wouldn't sit still for something like that. They'd retaliate. They'd make life hell for everybody involved."

Mig was right. The Nygaards had attitude, and enough money to swing it around like a high-powered weapon. Mig, his parents, even the Martinez family would suffer. Somehow.

"After my big confession, though," Mig added with an acerbic laugh, "my dad would probably say I deserved it."

Another nip to Jess's heart, when he realized how smoothly he'd sailed out of the closet compared with Mig. "You need to stop worrying about what he thinks. I don't know what we can do about Brandon—I'm sure we'll figure out some kind of payback that won't return to bite us—but right now you have to hold your head high and go about your life. *Your* life." He reached for Mig's fingers and curled his own around them. "And I'd like to go about your life with you."

Mig seemed to feel a lot better after that. Jess felt better too. Being forthright was, he knew, a staple of any sound relationship, and so far, he and Mig had managed to accumulate a batch of hard-earned gold stars.

They tried to figure out a tolerable living situation and decided on one that seemed like a win-win. Mig would get a room at the Breakers, but he and Jess would indeed use it primarily as a love nest. Mig would store most of his belongings and spend most of his free time at the Bonners'. The motel would simply give them a place to be alone together whenever they chose.

If Mig could find work in Madison, he'd move there with Jess in January.

They were arguing over whether or not Jess should pay part of Mig's motel rent when the doorbell chimed, a startling sound. Visitors rarely used the bell. Moreover, it was too late in the evening for any visitors, whether they were doorbell ringers or not.

Jess and Mig exchanged questioning looks tinctured with worry. Jess eased open the bedroom door and stood in front of it, listening. He heard his father's voice. Then another male voice that caused Mig to jerk him by the arm.

"My dad's here," he whispered.

"Don't stress out," Jess whispered back. "Remember, he can't make you do anything you don't want to do." Mig's kneejerk response was understandable. He'd just recently turned eighteen. The realization that your parents no longer had the power to order you around took some getting used to.

They both crept back to the door and listened.

Tom Finch had come to the Bonner house with both barrels blazing. What Jess heard made him wince, made his heart hurt. He felt far worse for Mig than he did for himself or his father, who not only kept his cool but said some of the most insightful things Jess had ever heard him say.

Mig, though, had his head and eyes lowered. He looked stricken. Jess hoped like hell he didn't regret outing himself, wouldn't be overwhelmed by guilt and go slinking back to his parents' house, where he'd have pretend he'd had a fit of temporary insanity that resulted in delusions of queerness.

Jess stepped behind Mig and wrapped both arms around him, resting his cheek against Mig's back. At first Mig didn't respond to the embrace. It was a frightening moment. But then he covered Jess's arms with his own, and added his own grip to Jess's hold, and it was obvious they were locking themselves together.

Soon, Tom Finch stopped hurling threats and insults. He didn't have much choice. Jim Bonner was giving him a polite but unbending version of the bum's rush, and Mig, from all indications, wasn't going anywhere except to the Bonners' sleeper sofa. It must have maddened Mr. Finch not to be able to dictate where and how Dylan lived. The guy was a bona fide control freak.

As his vehicle pulled out of the driveway, Jess asked, "How do you think your mother's going to take this?"

Mig turned to face him. "Hard."

"Think she'll call you?"

"Yeah. But it'll probably be after she gets back. I'm guessing my dad won't tell her 'til he picks her up from the airport. Maybe the day after tomorrow I'll go over there to pack up my stuff. She'll be home, but the old man should be at the shop." Anticipating the confrontation, Mig sighed. He sounded resigned when he spoke again. "We'll talk about it, but she won't really hear me. She'll cry. She'll want to sweep it all under the carpet."

Jess ran a hand over Mig's hair. "You're not going to do that, are you?"

Mig shook his head. Those dark strands, nearly dry now but charmingly messy, skated against Jess's palm. "No. I've waited too long for this." His smile was so tender, so full of appreciation and guarded optimism, Jess couldn't help but feel triumphant. For both of them.

"Come here," Jess said, drawing Mig into his arms.

"You're my freedom, Jesse."

The declaration solidified and rang in Jess's ears. *You're my freedom.* It was the phrase he'd almost spoken when they'd stood over that spaghetti loop and Jess had asked for a chance with him.

At that moment, all doubt fled. He knew.

This is right. This is what's enriching my life.

EPILOGUE

BIG and fluffy as goose down, the snowflakes had already piled up to a depth of three inches. Mig was arranging his book collection on the shelving unit Jess had given him for Christmas. Red had decorated its sides with a cartoon history of their relationship, starting on Sunrise Street, but he'd had to use a good deal of artistic license. He wasn't privy to most of what had gone on. Thank God.

Jess, lounging on the couch, alternately watched Mig and the falling snow. Their one-bedroom upper had a small porch off the living room, and it was through the glass storm door and the windows flanking it that Jess could gaze outside. Only a fireplace would've made the scene cozier. But you couldn't expect too many amenities for eight hundred bucks a month. Not in a place within walking distance of campus. In fact, they'd been lucky to find *anything* with off-street parking. Jess had left his rusty-trusty Ford behind in Cold Harbor, but Mig needed his truck to get to work.

Mig's phone made a trumpet fanfare sound. Since he was only wearing loose sweatpants, the phone wasn't in his pocket. He quickly looked around for it, then looked to Jess for help.

"I think it's in the bedroom," Jess said, admiring the view of half-clothed man. He watched his lover disappear down the short hallway.

They both worked out regularly now—not because they were vain, but because it excited the hell out of them to see and feel the solid contours of each other's body. Mig, who'd already had an edge in the physique department, looked hot as all freakin' irresistible hell with his clothes off. Sometimes Jess sprouted wood just thinking about him.

With a wistful smile, he went over to his desk, pulled the Jess-and-Mig treasure chest from the bottom drawer, and returned to the couch. The box was filling as rapidly with mementoes as the streets outside were with snow. Jess hadn't realized how sentimental he could be. But Mig had proved an even bigger softie. He'd squirreled away three times as much stuff as Jess had.

The handmade bracelet still lay inside, wrapped in a square of paper towel. Jess uncovered it just enough to reveal the central row of beads. Fondly, he ran a fingertip over them.

Mig had been perplexed by Tomby's gift. Although he'd been touched by the gesture and deeply moved by the bracelet's significance, he still felt ambivalent about the giver. He wasn't a grudge-holder, but he wasn't quite ready to put the piece on display. *"It's gonna be some time before we know if she's really changed,"* he'd said.

Jess couldn't fault him for his caution. When it came to expressions of feeling, Mig was anything but shallow and capricious. He placed a high premium on sincerity. So unless and until Tomby proved herself a better person, Mig wouldn't fully endow her gift with personal meaning.

After tucking the bracelet beneath the other contents of the box, Jess unfolded a letter he'd received from Joel, the one in which his big brother had responded to his Big Announcement.

Hey Midbro!

Guess what? Your news was not the huge hairy scary bulletin you thought it would be. Mom asked me about 4 years ago if I thought there was something 'different' about you and I said 'Well I think he's kind of an egghead and he might be gay, but aside from that he isn't too strange.' And guess what else? Mom said 'Thats pretty much what I think.' So there you go. We both kind of knew.

I figure next I'll get a letter from Mom telling me she was aducted (sp?) and knocked up by aliens and Red was the result. Look at it this way, at least no one can say the Bonner boys are ordinary. ☺

So your with Mig Finch now? You could of done a lot worse Jess. He's a nice kid and a 'handsome lad'. (Dont go reading nothing into that LOL!) I hope you guys are happy and never take no shit from nobody.

Joel went on to talk a little about DADT, how he didn't really care one way or another about it as long as he was serving with "good people." *Soldiers*, he'd written, *have to be soldiers first and everything else second. Thats all I give a rip about.*

Since Joel usually wrote a single letter to the whole family, this personal reply meant he'd taken Jess's coming-out seriously. His love and support shone through all the lighthearted understatement.

And their mother? All she'd said was, "Oh, I knew that years ago." And then she'd asked, "Nobody's kicked your butt yet, have they?"

Jess returned the chest to the drawer. Fragments of Mig's conversation floated from the bedroom. He couldn't have been talking to his new employer; it was too late in the day. He couldn't have been talking to an acquaintance; he and Jess had only just begun to meet people. Jess listened more carefully.

Ah, it was Mrs. Finch. Mig had reached an uneasy peace with his mother, although his father still refused to speak to him. In fact, Mig suspected his mom had to call him on the sly.

"She always goes with his program," Mig had said dejectedly last fall. "And after that, the church's."

Jess wasn't surprised. The Finches had always presented a united front, with each other and with the local Methodists. It must've been their way of showing their commitment to strong family values.

Ha.

Jess thought of the Nygaard and Martinez families, and of his own. Funny how kids always reflected their parents' standards, either through adoption of them or rebellion against them. Funny how those paths to acceptance or rejection could either be direct, with nary a detour, or meandering.

Bran had clearly absorbed his parents' priorities, which consisted of presenting an impressive appearance, always getting your way, and not giving a shit about other people unless they could advance your personal agenda.

Jess had seen him only once since moving to Madison, at the Rathskeller in the Student Union. Bran had abandoned the preppie image he'd briefly toyed with. Instead, he'd massaged his hipster look into righteous coolness—accessorized his meticulously casual clothing with hat and scarf and jewelry, put aside the contact lenses in favor of horn-rimmed glasses, coaxed his hair into a more relaxed position. But he obviously hadn't perfected his queerness. He'd been with a girl. Or, more accurately, his girlfriend, judging by the way he'd slung an arm over her shoulders and kept pulling her close to murmur in her ear.

That day, after Bran had fetched himself a steaming, oversized cup of designer coffee, Jess decided it was time to leave the Rat. He accidentally on purpose bumped into Bran and sent the hot beverage cascading down his belly and crotch. Bran screamed like a little boy and began cussing a blue streak in the same high-pitched voice. Jess, acting oblivious, his hat pulled over his head, hurried away and disappeared into the crowd. "Take that, you pretentious fuckin' asshole," he'd whispered.

Bran had never caught a good enough glimpse of him to recognize him.

Mig had been delighted to hear the story, and that alone made Jess's impetuous risk worthwhile.

The love of his life strolled back into the living room and stood over the couch. "That was my mother. She wanted to know if I needed anything. I didn't say what I was tempted to say."

"So she didn't ask if *we* needed anything?"

Mig leaned over the back of the couch. "You're shittin' me, right?"

"I assume she's still pretending I don't exist."

"Don't worry about it. *I* know you exist." Mig's smile was rueful, but only a little. "You know, you need to get off that gorgeous ass and start unpacking boxes." He playfully skimmed a hand over Jess's hair.

Jess grabbed his wrist and kissed the inside of it. "I can't. I'm paralyzed with serenity. Plus, the scenery's too fine."

"In other words, you're feeling lazy and getting horny."

"And *you're* really getting good with synonyms."

Grinning, Mig stood up. Jess's gaze again wandered to the windows. He sat on the edge of the couch cushion, poised to get up. "Hey, take off your pants and put on your shoes."

"If I do that, I won't have anything on except shoes." Mig gave him a puzzled, wary look. "Have you developed a new kink or something?"

"Just do it. Please?" Jess got up and peeled off his own sweats. Naked, he scurried to the apartment's entrance, which was in the kitchen, and slipped on his boots.

"You're serious," Mig said, following him.

"Of course I am. I'm a serious guy."

"Not always." Nevertheless, Mig stripped and got into his footwear. "Now what? Do we, like, dance down the stairway while singing show tunes?"

Jess took hold of Mig's hand and led him to the porch door. Darkness had settled over the city along with the snow. Jess opened

K. Z. SNOW

the storm door, then the screen door. A frosty line of white had spread between them.

"Come on," Jess said, urging Mig along. "This might not be the rooftop, but it's close."

That was when Mig got it. A growing smile cut into his cheeks.

Hand in hand, they stepped onto the porch and stood at the railing.

"Naked to the world!" Jess cried to the white-flecked sky.

They tilted up their faces and extended their linked hands above their heads.

"To the universe!" Mig shouted.

Laughing, they turned toward each other and into a warming embrace.

"What did you mean when you said I'm your freedom?" Jess asked.

Mig shivered against him, and Jess pressed closer, rubbing Mig's back. "This," Mig said.

Yes, exactly. This.

Jess kissed the side of Mig's cold face. "Seems love has a lot to recommend it."

"Seems it does." Mig curled tighter into him. "Uh, Jess?"

"Yeah?"

"I'm freezing my nuts off."

"Me too." *Can't let that happen.* "I think we've made our point."

210

If there's one thing K.Z. SNOW loves more than indulging her wayward imagination, it's the natural world and, especially, animals. She's been a companion to most domesticated creatures and a good number of the feral ones commonly known as men. After too many turbulent years, her life in the upper Midwest is finally boring as hell—an achievement as well as a blessing.

She's overeducated, underskilled, and has written a lot of stuff. Her only awards are two medals she received, obviously out of sympathy, for playing the bassoon and making it sound like a malfunctioning chainsaw.

Visit K.Z.'s blog at http://kzsnow.blogspot.com.